Creatures

Give a Dog a Bone

Louise Cooper

Scholastic Children's Books
Commonwealth House, 1–19 New Oxford Street,
London WC1A 1NU, UK
London ~ New York ~ Toronto ~ Sydney ~ Auckland
Mexico City ~ New Delhi ~ Hong Kong

First published by Scholastic Ltd, 1999

Text copyright © Louise Cooper, 1999

ISBN 0 439 01113 2

All rights reserved
Typeset by Falcon Oast Graphic Art
Printed by Cox & Wyman Ltd, Reading, Berks

2 4 6 8 10 9 7 5 3 1

1

As she climbed on board the coach with the rest of the school orchestra, Pippa Mitchell saw that Liddy Kovak had been crying. Liddy was trying to hide behind her long brown hair, but her eyes were red-rimmed and her cheeks looked puffy. Pippa dithered, wondering whether to say something. Before she could make up her mind, though, Liddy had slid past her and hurried to a seat as near the back as she could get.

"What's the matter with her, then?" someone stage-whispered loudly. Pippa turned to see Jayne Pickering staring after Liddy with nosey interest.

1

Pippa shrugged. "I didn't get the chance to ask."

"Well, I don't suppose it's anything interesting. It wouldn't be with Liddy, after all. Come on, let's sit here, well away from her." Before Pippa could say a word, Jayne elbowed her into the nearest pair of seats, plonking herself down next to the aisle. Pippa was annoyed. She didn't particularly like Jayne, and would rather have chosen someone else to sit next to. But the coach was filling up now, and it was too late to argue.

Jayne, though, wasn't really interested in Pippa. She was craning out into the aisle to watch the door, and as a tall, dark boy got on to the coach, her eyes lit up.

"Hi, Chris!" Jayne waved, tossing her blonde hair back in an exaggerated gesture that she'd spent ages practising in front of a mirror. "I saved a seat for you!"

She pointed to the empty places opposite theirs. But Chris Ambrose took no notice. He was peering towards the back of the coach, and his face was concerned.

"What's up with Liddy?" he asked. "She's been crying."

"I know," said Pippa. "I was going to ask her, but—"

"I'll go and talk to her." Chris flicked Pippa a quick smile. "See you."

Jayne scowled as he went and sat down next to Liddy. Then, as the doors shut with a hiss and the coach started to move, she slumped back in her seat to sulk.

Pippa grinned to herself. Jayne was always trying to get Chris's attention, and it was howlingly obvious that he wasn't interested. Jayne's problem, Pippa reflected cattily, was that Chris was too nice to want to hang around with her.

The coach turned out into the main road, and, ignoring Jayne, Pippa looked through the window. They'd be out of the city soon, and she savoured the thought of the excitement that lay ahead. The school orchestra – forty players and all their instruments – was heading for the Cotswolds, to play at the Low Aspen music festival. Pippa had been looking forward to the festival for months, ever since the news came that they'd been invited to take part.

They were to play in four concerts – and, best of all, they'd be staying at Aspen Manor itself. The Manor sounded pretty amazing: a huge country house in its own grounds, with loads of rooms, banqueting hall, the lot. In term time it was a college or something (Pippa couldn't quite remember), but every August holiday it became the festival headquarters, and a lot of the visiting musicians would be staying there.

Pippa was busy imagining what Aspen Manor would be like when Jayne's voice interrupted.

"She's started snivelling again." Jayne was peering back at Liddy. "As if she wasn't enough of a mess to start with!"

Pippa eyed her suspiciously. "What's that supposed to mean?"

"Well, *look* at her. She obviously didn't even bother to wash her hair before she came. And those *clothes*! She'll show us all up at the festival."

"Oh, shut up, Jayne!" Pippa said angrily. "Leave her alone." It was hardly Liddy's fault if she had weird parents who didn't let her wear fashionable clothes, or go out with friends, or even ask friends round to her place. OK, she was a bit strange – hard to talk to, and she didn't join in things. But she was one of the best musicians in the whole orchestra. That was why Chris liked her.

Jayne was still staring – or glaring – at Liddy. Pippa opened her mouth again to tell her to give it a rest, then sighed, changing her mind. *Forget it, Pippa*, she told herself. *Just concentrate on enjoying yourself. That's what this is supposed to be about, after all.*

At the first sight of Aspen Manor, any thoughts about Jayne or Liddy flew straight out of Pippa's head.

The house certainly *was* amazing. Half of it looked mediaeval, while the other half was like something out of a gothic horror movie: all tall chimneys and gables, with ivy covering the walls. Pippa stood and stared at it in awe, while everyone else climbed off the coach and Mr Elwood, their conductor, and Ms Lane, the senior music teacher, supervised the unloading of instruments from the depths of the luggage compartment. There was an awful thump and twang as a cello slipped, and Mr Elwood yelled, "Be *careful* with that!"

Chris appeared beside Pippa. He grinned and held up his oboe case.

"Glad I haven't got to lug anything bigger than this!"

"Me, too," Pippa grinned back, tapping her violin.

Everyone was off the coach now, and they all headed for the house and went in at the front door. Inside was an enormous entrance hall, with an imposing staircase and three passages leading from it.

"Wow!" Pippa goggled. "It's like a maze!"

"It was a monastery once," Chris said. "Then in Victorian times some rich local guy rebuilt it, and his family lived here."

"Just one family?" Pippa marvelled at the thought. "It's *huge* – they must have rattled around in it! *And* got lost," she added.

Chris grinned again. "We'll probably get lost, too. Could be a laugh."

Mr Elwood was calling people over to the reception desk. As they joined the queue Pippa saw Liddy in the crowd, and she nudged Chris's arm. "Did you find out what she's upset about?"

"Yeah." Chris's face clouded. "You know how much she likes animals? Well, she found this abandoned dog a few days ago. She really fell in love with it; wanted to keep it."

Pippa began to get the picture. "Her folks wouldn't let her?"

"Right. They wouldn't even talk about it. They took it to the RSPCA and told them to 'get rid of it'."

"That's disgusting!" said Pippa.

"Yeah, and pretty typical, from what Liddy said. She thought the RSPCA were going to put it to sleep. I told her they won't, they'll find it a good home, but I don't think she believes me. She's really down about it."

"Poor Liddy!" Pippa's family had one dog, two cats and four rabbits, and she found it hard to imagine what parents like Liddy's must be like.

They moved on to the desk, where Mr Elwood and some people from the festival staff were handing out door keys.

"Ah, Pippa," said Mr Elwood. "You're in number thirty-seven, with . . . let me see . . ." He consulted a list. "Ah, yes. With Jayne Pickering—"

Pippa's spirits crashed to the ground. "Oh, but—"

– "and Liddy Kovak."

Jayne *and* Liddy? It had to be the worst combination in the entire world!

"Mr Elwood," Pippa said desperately, "couldn't I—"

"What's that?" Mr Elwood was besieged by people and didn't have the patience to listen. "Yes, of course someone'll show you where the room is; nobody expects you to find your way around on your own yet. Here's your key; here you are, take it, take it!"

And he turned to the next person in the queue before Pippa could say another word.

The room the three girls were given over-looked Aspen Manor's grounds, which were mostly smooth, rolling lawns with shrubberies, clumps of trees and, off to one side, a sunken garden with a fishpond in the middle. Beyond the wall and down a winding hill the rooftops of Low Aspen, the old market town, were just visible.

While Pippa unpacked (if she didn't make herself do it now, she never would), Jayne bagged the dressing-table mirror and started experimenting with hair styles. Liddy just stood silently at the window, staring out.

"I'm going downstairs to have a look round," Pippa ventured at last. "Want to come, Liddy?"

"No." Liddy shook her head without turning round.

"Oh. Right. Jayne . . .?" Well, she had to ask, didn't she?

"I'm too busy," said Jayne, admiring her reflection.

Pippa left them to it. If they started quarrelling the moment she was out of sight, that was their problem, not hers.

She only got lost three times on her way back to the main hall, which wasn't bad going. Outside, another coach had arrived and a crowd of people all speaking French were

8

climbing off. Pippa crunched across the gravel, and wandered round to the side of the house, where the sunken garden was.

The garden was surrounded by a low wall, like a parapet, and worn brick steps led down to it. As she went down the steps Pippa saw that the garden was very neglected. The lilies in the pond were so overgrown that you could only see about half the water, and the flower beds were full of weeds. At the far end a stone statue rose out of the tangle, and Pippa walked over to have a closer look.

The statue was a life-size carving of a man wearing Victorian clothes. He stood facing the house, his thumbs pushed into the lapels of his coat, giving him a self-important air that made Pippa want to giggle. At his feet, standing alert and with mouth open and tongue lolling, was a dog. It was a bit like a Staffordshire terrier, very bow-legged, and it looked as haughty as its master.

The stonework was covered with lichen, but the letters of an inscription were just visible through the green fuzz on the plinth. Pippa bent to look more closely.

NATHANIEL THORNBURY, the words began; **1787** . . . Then the moss became thicker and the rest of the date was obscured.

Underneath, it said something about "gratitude of the parish" and "charitable and benevolent works" but, again, she couldn't make out any more.

Then, under the statue of the dog, she saw that there was another, smaller inscription.

"**LANCER** . . ." Pippa read aloud to herself – and frowned. *What* did the rest of it say? It looked like just three words.

"**FAITHFUL BEYOND DEATH**".

"Strange, isn't it?"

The voice from behind made Pippa jump, and she spun round to see Chris walking towards her.

"Sorry." He raised both hands in a peace-making gesture. "Didn't mean to scare you, but I was looking at that a few minutes ago. What do you make of it?"

"It's weird," Pippa said. "I mean, *beyond* death?"

"Yeah, exactly. What's it getting at?" Crouching down, Chris rubbed at the moss with his thumb, trying to clear it away. "I bet there's a story in there somewhere."

Pippa grinned. "You're not scared of it, are you?"

"No-o. But . . . those words *are* sort of creepy. Almost like a threat."

"A *threat?* Who to?"

"Oh, I dunno. Anyone who upsets the dog's master, maybe?" Chris was looking embarrassed by this time, and Pippa laughed.

"Well, Lancer *and* his master have both been dead for ages. So we're not very likely to go upsetting either of them!"

Chris paused, then suddenly he laughed, too. "Yeah. You're right; it's just me being stupid. Don't take any notice."

"Don't worry," said Pippa. "I never take any notice of you anyway!"

She dodged the swipe he aimed at her, and they walked back up the steps and towards the house. As they went, Pippa looked over her shoulder – and saw something that made her hesitate. There was someone in the nearby shrubbery, standing very still and staring down into the sunken garden. The sun was in Pippa's eyes and she couldn't see very clearly.

But she thought the figure was Liddy.

2

"It's all right for you," Jayne grumbled as she and Pippa went downstairs to breakfast the next morning. "You just went on snoring. *I* was the one who was kept awake half the night!"

"Oh, stop exaggerating!" said Pippa. "I bet it wasn't any more than a few minutes. And I don't snore!" she added indignantly.

"You do. So what with you on one side, and *her* snivelling and snuffling on the other—"

"Ask to be moved to another room, then," Pippa interrupted. She'd had enough of Jayne's moans and groans; they were spoiling what would otherwise have been a perfect summer morning. As they walked into the huge, panelled dining hall – the refectory, it was officially called – she added, "You're so selfish. You ought to feel sorry for Liddy after what her parents did. No wonder she was crying!"

"What, over some stupid dog?" Jayne turned up her nose. "It's hardly the end of the world, is it? Anyway, I bet it had fleas."

With that remark she stalked off to find a chair as near to Chris as she could manage. Pippa was only too glad to let her go. If Jayne didn't ask to be moved to another room, she thought, *she* just might.

Breakfast was enormous, and as good as last night's dinner had been. By the time she'd waded through her plateful, Pippa was ready for a morning flopped out in the sun doing nothing. Her luck was out. As the meal was being cleared away, Mr Elwood got to his feet.

"Right, you lot," he announced. "Rehearsal in half an hour!"

There was a barrage of groans from the tables, which Mr Elwood silenced by clapping his hands.

"All *right*! I know it's your first day, but we're not here on holiday. And we need to do a *lot* of work on 'Greensleeves' – it still sounds like a cats' chorus!" He paused. "But seeing as the weather's so good, we'll practise outside. Get yourselves organized, and gather in the sunken garden. You've now got precisely twenty-eight minutes!"

Reluctantly they all went to fetch their instruments. To Pippa's surprise, Jayne hurried to catch up with Liddy as they started to climb the stairs. Pippa thought for a moment that Jayne must have taken some notice of what she'd said before breakfast, but then she heard Jayne's voice.

"A cats' chorus, d'you think, Liddy? Or is it more like a dog whimpering?"

Liddy tensed as if she'd been stung, and Jayne's laughter carried clearly above the general chatter as she hurried on ahead.

Pippa stared after Jayne. She wanted to slap her face. She also wanted to say something to Liddy – tell her to take no notice and not to let it get to her. But Jayne had disappeared round the curve of the stairs, and Liddy had hunched up like a tortoise going into its shell. Pippa sighed, and decided that it was probably wiser to do nothing at all.

When the morning's rehearsal got going, it didn't take Pippa long to realize that Jayne had it in for Liddy in a big way. If there was any chance to be unpleasant, Jayne took it. She whispered nasty comments about Liddy's hair and clothes. She kept making remarks, much more loudly, about dogs. And twice she deliberately nudged the back of Liddy's chair during quiet pieces of music, so that the chair rocked and Liddy's flute squeaked off key. The first time it happened, Mr Elwood glared at Liddy. The second time, he glared *and* made a growling noise in his throat.

Then Jayne did it again, so hard that Liddy dropped her flute. They were practising the troublesome "Greensleeves"; it ground to a halt amid a background of giggles, and Mr Elwood sighed loudly.

"Lydia!" There was a new outburst of sniggering as he used Liddy's full name, which everyone knew she hated. "I'm sure you're as bored with this piece as the rest of us, but if you would kindly make *some* attempt to concentrate, we might stand a chance of getting to the end of it!"

Liddy turned as red as a beetroot and looked as if she'd burst into tears at any moment. Pippa could have thrown Jayne into the pond.

"Well," Mr Elwood went on sourly, "now that Lydia's managed to disrupt us for the third time, I suppose we might as well take a break.

Twenty minutes. And when we start again, there'd better be some improvement!"

He stomped off up the steps and out of the sunken garden. As Pippa put her violin down, she saw Liddy get up and walk away from the rows of chairs. Carrying her flute and her music, she went over to the statue. For a few moments she stood looking down at the stone dog; then she sat down in the grass, bent over the music and started to play.

"*Now* what's she doing?" Jayne demanded.

"Practising the bit you kept making her mess up," said Pippa sharply.

Jayne shrugged. "If she can't take a joke, bad luck! Have we all got to sit here listening to her playing the same stupid notes over and over again, till she *does* manage to get it right?"

Pippa turned angrily on her. "Look, cut it out, will you? You've been trying to wind Liddy up since rehearsal started. Just leave her alone!"

Jayne smiled sweetly. "Or what?" she asked.

She went off to join a group – including Chris – who had strolled over to the pond. Pippa stared after her, seething. Trouble was, Jayne was right; she couldn't actually *do* anything to stop her having a go at Liddy. With a self-pitying sigh Pippa shut her violin in its case, then stretched, yawned and sat back on her chair.

After a couple of minutes Chris moved away from the group by the pond and went off on his own. Jayne promptly followed him, and Pippa sighed again. Jayne still hadn't got the message that she wasn't exactly Chris's favourite person. That was at the root of her animosity towards Liddy – the fact that Chris liked her got right up Jayne's nose. With any luck, Pippa hoped, Chris might tell her what he *really* thought before too long.

She shut her eyes, enjoying the sunshine. But it wasn't long before the sounds of an argument interrupted her daydreams.

The noise was coming from the direction of the statue, and as Pippa sat up she heard Liddy's voice.

"Give it back to me! It isn't yours – oh, don't!"

Liddy and Jayne were facing each other by the statue. Jayne had Liddy's flute in her hand. She must have crept up on her and snatched it, and as Liddy tried to grab it back she held it out of reach.

"*Don't!*" Liddy pleaded again. "If you break it, I'll never be able to have another one!"

"Fine with me!" Jayne retorted. "We might all get some peace and quiet!"

Others were watching now, but nobody did anything to help Liddy. To them, the argument was just a bit of a laugh.

Someone, though, didn't find it funny. Suddenly a voice called sharply, "Jayne, stop pratting around!" and Chris came down the steps at the far end of the garden. He looked furious and disgusted, and as Jayne saw him her face turned red.

"Give it back to her," Chris said, very quietly. "She's right; it's not yours. And if you *do* break it, you'll screw up the festival for everyone. Is that what you want?"

Jayne was crimson by now. "It's only a *joke*," she said sulkily.

"Great. So the joke's over. Give it back, OK?"

Jayne was so humiliated that for a moment Pippa thought she really would break the flute. But Chris had defeated her. If she didn't do what he said, she'd show herself up as a sulky brat; and above all she didn't want that.

But she wasn't going to give in completely. Whirling, she took two strides to the statue, and shoved Liddy's flute into the stone dog's open mouth.

18

"Give it to Fido, why don't we?" she said pettishly. "See if *he* can play it properly!"

For one glorious second Pippa imagined the stone figure of Lancer coming to life and biting a very large chunk out of Jayne's hand. It didn't, of course. It was only a statue.

But there *was* an odd coincidence. As Jayne pushed the flute into Lancer's mouth, a gust of wind blew across the garden, and the flute made a sound, like a soft, distant whistle. It must have been the wind that did it. But just for a moment it sounded as if it was coming from somewhere else – somewhere much further away.

Jayne swung round and, with what dignity she could salvage, stamped back to her place in the orchestra. Everyone looked at her. No one said anything. Then Liddy went quietly up to the statue and took the flute. She laid one hand on the stone dog's head, and patted it. And she murmured something. Pippa thought it was: "Thanks, Lancer. . ."

And the wind – it *must* have been the wind – made the flute whistle again. The same strange note. Faraway. Haunting.

As Liddy walked away, Pippa continued to stare at the stone dog. There seemed to be something *different* about it. It was only her imagination, of course, or the angle of the sun had changed.

But she could have sworn that Lancer's head had turned just a fraction, and that his stone eyes were gazing after Liddy's departing back.

3

There were no rehearsals that afternoon and everyone could do whatever they liked. Pippa was delighted – a few hours' lazing around was exactly what she needed, and she was soon relaxing with sunglasses, sunblock and a magazine on the lawn of the Manor garden.

She'd finished reading the magazine and was enjoying a delicious daydream when she heard footsteps approaching. Then someone plonked down on the grass next to her.

"Hi," said Chris. "Studying hard for the next rehearsal?"

Pippa stuck her tongue out without bothering to open her eyes.

"I've been talking to a couple of people who work here," Chris went on. "Found out something interesting."

"Mmm?"

"About the guy in that statue, and his dog."

That *did* catch Pippa's attention, and she sat up, pulling off her shades. "What's the story?"

"Apparently it's the same guy who rebuilt the Manor a hundred years ago," Chris told her. "Nathaniel Thornbury. He was some sort of big cheese in the area; did a lot of good works – you know, helping the poor and all that kind of Victorian benefactor stuff. Anyway, he had this dog, Lancer. They were real mates, went everywhere together, and when Lancer died, Nathaniel had him buried in the churchyard. Then when *he* died, he said in his will that he wanted to be buried right next to his dog."

"Was he?" Pippa asked.

Chris nodded. "Their graves are side by side, down at Low Aspen church. But you haven't heard the *really* interesting bit yet. There's another story about Lancer." He paused, looking mysterious. "One night, Nathaniel and his servants were asleep when the Manor kitchen caught fire. They might all have been killed, but Nathaniel was woken up by the sound of

Lancer barking. He smelled the smoke, raised the alarm, and they managed to put the fire out before anyone got hurt or the house burned down."

"I've heard of dogs doing that sort of thing," said Pippa, nodding.

"Yeah, me too. But there's one big difference. When that fire happened, Lancer had been dead for years."

Pippa stared at him, wide-eyed. "Then it was—"

"Lancer's ghost, warning his old master. That's why Nathaniel had that inscription put on the statue."

Faithful Beyond Death. It made sense now, and Pippa shivered. "That's *spooky*," she said. Then she frowned as an unnerving thought occurred to her. She almost didn't want to say it, but forced herself. "Do you think . . . the ghost ever comes back now?"

"I shouldn't think so," said Chris. "I mean, Lancer came to save Nathaniel, didn't he? He wouldn't be interested in anyone else." He paused. "Why? Do you know something I don't?"

Pippa laughed. "'Course not!" But the laugh didn't sound very convincing. For some reason she couldn't stop herself from thinking about

Jayne, and Liddy's flute, and a strange, distant whistle.

And suddenly the garden didn't seem quite such a sunny place any more.

On her way up to bed that night, Pippa kept looking over her shoulder. It was stupid, of course – just because she'd heard a creepy story, she was imagining spooks everywhere. There'd been nothing weird about the atmosphere in Aspen Manor last night, and there was nothing weird about it now. She was being an idiot, scaring herself for no good reason. Anyway, why should anyone be frightened of Lancer's ghost? He sounded like a pretty great dog to have around.

All the same, she lay awake for a long time after the light was switched off, trying to tell herself that the faint sounds she could hear were just the ordinary noises that a very old house made. You noticed them more at night, that was all. There really was no reason to get the wind up.

She did get to sleep at last. But not for long. At two o'clock in the morning, a muttering voice woke her up.

Pippa opened bleary eyes, blinking at the darkness (nights were much darker in the country than in the city, she'd discovered) and trying to work out where the muttering was coming from. Behind her, it sounded like. . .

She turned over and raised herself on her elbows. She could vaguely make out the other two beds, Jayne's nearer to her and Liddy's on the far side of the room. All was quiet in Liddy's corner. But Jayne was tossing and turning under her duvet, and it was her voice that had woken Pippa.

"*Mnnh. . .*" Jayne mumbled. "*Uhh . . . goaway, goaWAY!*"

"Jayne?" Pippa hissed. "Jayne!"

A sigh came from Liddy's bed, but she didn't wake up. Jayne started to kick, as if she was cycling. "*No-o-o. . .*" she whimpered. "*No, don't . . . Mmmmpf . . . don't want to. . .*"

She was obviously having a nightmare. After what had happened this morning Pippa was half tempted to leave her to it, but her conscience twinged. Nightmares were horrible, and Jayne sounded really frightened. So Pippa got up and padded over to Jayne's bed.

"Jayne," she whispered. "Jayne, wake up."

"*N-n-n-nh!*" Jayne kicked again and the duvet slid on to the floor. Pippa picked it up, then gently shook Jayne's shoulder. "*Jayne!* Come on, it's only a dream. Wake up, will you?"

But still Jayne didn't wake. She only went on mumbling and whimpering, and Pippa was baffled. Whatever was the matter with her? Why wouldn't she come out of it?

A queasy, worried little feeling nagged at Pippa, and she hurried over to Liddy's bed and grabbed the dim hump of her shoulder.

"Liddy, it's me, Pippa. There's something the matter with Jayne. She's having a bad dream, and I can't. . ."

The words tailed off. Pippa had been shaking Liddy's shoulder – or what she thought was her shoulder. But it felt much too squashy. Not like a person at all. In fact—

She pulled back Liddy's duvet.

Liddy wasn't in the bed. What Pippa had been shaking was just a pillow, carefully arranged so that it looked, in the gloom, as if someone was lying there.

Slowly, Pippa straightened up. Where was Liddy? OK, maybe she couldn't sleep or something; maybe Jayne's muttering had disturbed her and she'd gone off to get away from it. But why set up the pillow to make it look as if she was still here?

Jayne made a frightened little squeaking noise – then her muttering stopped. When Pippa went to look at her again, she was lying still and quiet and peaceful, as if the nightmare had never happened.

This was weird. Liddy missing, Jayne having horrible dreams that suddenly went away . . . What on earth was going on?

Confused, and uncertain of what to do, Pippa was standing dithering in the middle of the floor when she heard a sound from outside. It was a long way off, and very faint, but it sounded like someone whistling on a long, rising note. Startled, she ran to the window, pulled back the curtain and looked outside.

The sky was clear and the moon strong enough to cast shadows, so the nearest section of the Manor garden was fairly visible. Nothing was moving out there. Pippa's gaze scanned across the lawn, past clumps of bushes (they seemed to be moving, but it was only the breeze) and on to the sunken garden. This was harder to see clearly; the moonlight didn't quite reach it, and all she could make out was a dark smudge of overgrown greenery, the glimmer of the pond, and the pale blob of Nathaniel Thornbury's statue beyond.

Something different about the statue . . . Pippa stood very still as she remembered that peculiar little incident this morning, when she'd thought that Lancer's head had moved a fraction. She peered harder, trying to separate the figure of the dog from that of his master. She couldn't actually *see* Lancer. Maybe he was hidden by a bush or a clump of tall grass. But from here, it looked as if there *was* no dog next to Nathaniel.

Then she heard the whistle again. It was so sudden, and so much closer than last time, that it made her jump, and her teeth snapped together painfully. What the heck *was* that? No one in their right mind would be wandering around in the middle of the night, whistling, as if they were calling a . . .

Dog . . .?

A horrible feeling lurched in Pippa's stomach, making her wish she hadn't eaten so much at dinner, as a scary possibility slipped into her mind. That sound had seemed, to her overworked imagination, to come from the sunken garden. Was it, *could* it be, the ghost of Nathaniel Thornbury, whistling to his faithful pet?

She dropped the curtain as if it were red-hot, ran back across the floor and threw herself into bed. She desperately wanted to put the light on, but she couldn't remember where the switch was, and she huddled under the duvet, fighting back panic. *That whistling's only a bird,* she tried to tell herself. *An owl, or something. Or if it IS a person, it's somebody alive and real. It isn't a ghost. It isn't, it ISN'T.*

Then she heard another noise. Very slight, very furtive. The noise of someone, or something, moving.

Right outside the bedroom door.

Pippa raised her head and peered over the edge of the duvet, her eyes wide and staring and her heart bumping so hard that she could feel it against her ribs. *What was that faint rattle?* Was it the doorknob? Was it turning? If only she could *see!* But at the same time she didn't want to see. She didn't want to know. She didn't want this to be happening to her . . .

With a creak, the dark shape of the door swung open, and it was all Pippa could do to stop herself from screaming at the top of her voice. Her teeth clamped on the duvet, biting hard to choke back the panic –

And her terror collapsed into astonished relief as she saw who was sneaking into the room.

"*Liddy!*" Pippa shot bolt upright.

"Shh!" Liddy put a finger to her lips. "You'll wake Jayne up."

29

Pippa scrambled out of bed. "I've just been *trying* to wake her; she was having a nightmare, but I couldn't – oh, never mind that now! Where have you been?"

Liddy shrugged. She was holding something in her hand, but in the gloom Pippa couldn't make out what it was. "I couldn't sleep, that's all. So I got up and walked around for a bit."

She was fully dressed, Pippa saw. Why had she bothered? The house was very warm.

"Did you go outside?"

There was a pause. Then: "No," said Liddy.

She was lying. Pippa knew it as surely as she knew anything. But why? What did she want to hide?

Liddy walked over to Jayne's bed. She didn't say anything; she just stared down at her for a few moments. Then she went to her own bed and, still in her clothes, slid under the duvet. "'Night," she said, and turned to face the wall.

Pippa sat staring at her, her mind boiling with questions. Why had Liddy fixed her bed to look as if she was in it when she wasn't? Why had she lied about going outside?

And why had she taken that object with her? Because Pippa could see what it was now. Liddy had put it down on a shelf where the moonlight reached, and the mystery of the whistling sound she'd heard was solved.

But another mystery had come to take its place. The mystery of what on earth Liddy had been doing, playing her flute out there in the garden, in the middle of the night.

4

"As if it wasn't enough to have a lousy night with awful dreams, and then waking up with a headache, and now I can't find my blue *tights*!" Jayne was working up to a classic tantrum as she scrabbled in suitcase, rucksack and bedside drawers all at the same time. "Where *are* they?"

"Try under the bed," Pippa suggested. "That's where mine usually end up."

"Yeah, well yours *would*, wouldn't they?" All the same, Jayne got down on her hands and knees and peered under her bed. "There's something there . . ." She reached, grunting, then stopped. "What the hell . . .?"

Her arm reappeared. She was grasping something. She looked at it – and squealed.

"*Uggh!*" With a violent movement Jayne flung the thing away from her. "It's *horrible!* Oh, yuk; oh my God!"

"What?" Pippa came scrambling over. "What is it? What have you found?"

"*That!*" Jayne pointed with a shaking finger. "Take it away from me, take it *away!*"

"It" was a bone. It was about as long as Pippa's forearm, elbow to wrist, with a rounded, knuckly bit at either end. It was very clean, very smooth, and a horrible, pallid whitish-yellow colour.

"Take it away!" Jayne repeated. "Just get it out of my sight!"

"Calm down!" Pippa said. "It's only a bone. The way you're going on, anyone'd think you'd found a rattlesnake under there!"

"*Only* a bone?" Jayne shrieked. "Who put it there? If it's their idea of a joke, it isn't *funny!*"

Pippa sighed, and picked up the bone with two fastidious fingers. "All right, all right, I'll take it away for you if you're so squeamish! And no, I haven't got the foggiest who did it. It certainly wasn't me."

She went out, leaving Jayne still sitting on the floor and shuddering. In the corridor, she met Liddy coming back from the bathroom.

And a thought occurred to her.

"Liddy," Pippa held the bone up. "Do you know anything about this?"

Liddy looked at the bone and frowned. "A bone? Whatever are you doing with it?"

"Jayne just found it under her bed. Someone must have put it there, and she isn't laughing." Pippa paused. "Well? Was it you?"

"*Me?*" Liddy looked astonished. "Don't be crazy! Why would I do anything so weird?"

"You and Jayne had that row yesterday."

"I know, but if I wanted to get back at her, I'd do something a bit better than *that*. That's just stupid." Liddy sighed. "She probably put it there herself, to get attention or something."

She had a point, Pippa thought. It was the sort of petty thing Jayne would do. Maybe she wanted Liddy to get the blame – another one of her spiteful little jabs . . .

"Look, I'm going downstairs; I'll take it and dump it for you if you want," Liddy offered.

Pippa nodded. "OK. Thanks." She handed it over. "Honestly, the fuss Jayne made, I thought she'd found something lethal under there!"

Liddy weighed the bone in her hand. Her eyes were suddenly very inward-looking.

"*One* bone can't hurt anyone," she said.

It was very strange, the way she emphasized the word "one". But before Pippa could ask what she meant, Liddy had walked away.

Jayne, of course, wanted to change rooms. When she found she couldn't, she made an enormous fuss about it and demanded that Pippa should swop beds with her.

"I know *she* put that bone there," she muttered darkly. "And I'm not going to sleep in the bed next to hers for another single night! It's all right for you; you're so thick-skinned that things like that don't bother you."

"Thanks a bunch!" said Pippa indignantly.

"Well, it's true; anyone can see it. So I want to swop beds."

Pippa couldn't be bothered to argue. It made no difference to her which bed she slept in, and if it helped keep the peace, fair enough. She didn't believe that Liddy had anything to do with the bone business, but there was no point trying to convince Jayne, so she let the subject drop. How the bone *had* got there, of course, was still a puzzle. But it hardly seemed to matter.

The orchestra had another rehearsal that morning. Jayne didn't try any sly tricks on

Liddy, but Pippa had an uneasy feeling that that wouldn't last. Jayne was good at bearing grudges, and knowing her, she was probably plotting something. Only next time, she'd make sure no one saw her doing it.

The rehearsal went a lot better today, and Mr Elwood was pleased with everyone's efforts. Again they had the afternoon off, and a crowd of them, including Pippa, decided to go in to Low Aspen to have a look around. Jayne had gone off somewhere on her own, but Chris was among the group – and so, to everyone's surprise, was Liddy.

The little town was a mile from the Manor, at the bottom of a long lane that wound steeply downhill. High hedges grew on either side of the lane, filled with wild flowers and grasses, and in among the hedges were groups of trees whose branches almost met overhead, turning the way into a green, shady tunnel.

Liddy dawdled, keeping away from the main group and dropping behind after a while. She was picking flowers, which she shouldn't have done, but when someone told her so she just shrugged and carried on. After that, they left her alone.

They passed a crossroads, then there was

another, shorter hill, and suddenly the lane opened out into a green triangle planted with flowers, with a church to one side and a long street of ancient buildings to the other.

"Real picture-postcard stuff, isn't it?" Chris said to Pippa. "No wonder all the tourists love it!"

"Yeah." Pippa was looking at the church. "Is that where Nathaniel Whatsit and his dog are buried?"

"Must be," said Chris. "Want to take a look?"

"No." She shook her head. "Not really." Or maybe she did, but on her own. Not with anyone else around. "I'm going to check out the shops," she told him. "I want to get a souvenir for Mum."

Chris raised his eyebrows. "Got a few hundred quid on you? It's all antiques and arty stuff, by the look of it."

"Oh, well. No harm in trying, is there? See you later."

The shops were expensive all right. About the only thing Pippa could have afforded was a *very* small china honey pot with a revoltingly kitsch bumble bee sitting on the lid. Mum would probably throw up at the sight of it, so she gave up the idea of souvenirs, bought herself an ice-cream and wandered back to the church. Reaching it, she looked over the wall. A Japanese family were there, taking photographs, but there was no sign of any of her schoolmates. OK then, she thought. Just a quick look.

The churchyard wasn't very big, so it didn't take long to find Nathaniel Thornbury's grave. There was a large and grandiose headstone, carved with a long list of all Nathaniel's good works. Beside it, much smaller but equally ornate, was the grave of the faithful Lancer.

On Lancer's grave lay a bunch of freshly picked wild flowers.

Pippa's eyes narrowed as she looked at the flowers. So that was why Liddy had been so keen to pick them! She must have known about the grave – either Chris had told her or she'd found it out for herself – and she'd been planning to visit it. It was probably the only reason why she'd come on this walk.

So why had Liddy wanted to put flowers on Lancer's grave? OK, she was upset about the dog she hadn't been allowed to keep. But surely there had to be more to it than that?

Raising her head, Pippa scanned the churchyard. The Japanese family had gone, but by the gate she saw Chris with a couple of other people from the orchestra, and on impulse she ran over to them.

"Chris, have you seen Liddy around?"

"No," said Chris. "Why?"

"It's –" She hesitated, aware that the others were listening. For some reason she didn't want them all to know. "Look, come over here a minute," she told Chris. "There's something I want to show you."

Chris followed her to the two graves. "Oh, you found it, then. . ." he started to say as he saw Nathaniel's headstone. Then he stopped, looking at the flowers. "Ah. They're the ones Liddy picked, aren't they?" He sighed. "Poor Liddy. She can't stop hurting about that dog."

"I think there's more to it," said Pippa.

He frowned. "What do you mean?"

Good question. But now she'd started, Pippa couldn't back off. And Chris, out of everyone she knew, was the most likely person to listen.

She took a deep breath. "Remember when we first saw the statue in the sunken garden? You said you thought it was creepy."

Chris looked at her uneasily. "Sure." He licked his lips. "But that was before I found out what the inscription meant. Anyway, it was only a sort of joke."

"Sort of?" Pippa challenged. "I don't think

so. Something about that statue *did* give you the creeps, didn't it? Just like it did me?"

Chris didn't answer straight away. He was thinking, and his expression was suddenly cautious. Pippa waited, and at last he said, "Look . . . promise you're not going to laugh?"

"I won't laugh."

"OK." It was Chris's turn to breathe deeply. "Well, last night I was having trouble sleeping. Strange place, really dark and quiet – you know what it's like. I was lying in bed when I heard this noise outside. It sounded like someone whistling."

Pippa's spine prickled sharply. "Go on," she said.

"I got up and looked out of the window. From the room I'm in you can see the sunken garden, and for a minute I thought there was somebody out there. There wasn't; it was just the statue, and I'd mistaken it for a real person. But. . ."

He paused, and Pippa realized that he didn't want to tell her the rest.

"Chris," she said quietly, "I am *not* going to laugh. OK?"

Chris bit his lip, then his shoulders heaved. "OK. But it sounds totally stupid. There's

Nathaniel's statue, right? And Lancer's next to him. Well, I could see them both clearly from my window."

He hesitated again, then with an effort turned to face Pippa. He looked embarrassed. And he also looked frightened.

"I wasn't dreaming," he said, "and I didn't imagine it. The moon was out and the statues had shadows. The statue of Lancer was completely still; I mean, it's made of stone, so of course it was. But . . ." He swallowed. "Honest, Pippa, I'm not joking. Lancer's shadow was *moving*."

5

"All right," Chris said as he and Pippa walked up the hill, out of earshot of the rest of the group. "Let's go through what we know." He started to count things off on his fingers. "Jayne had nightmares. Liddy went off somewhere with her flute, and that must have been the whistling we both heard. And I saw the shadow of Lancer's statue moving."

"I didn't," Pippa put in. "Though from my window I couldn't see the sunken garden as well as you."

"Right. First thing, then – shadows don't come to life and walk on their own. So it had to be a trick of the moonlight, and it fooled me."

Pippa nodded. They'd already agreed that any other possibility was far too crazy to believe. "But what about the bone under Jayne's bed?" she said.

Chris hesitated. "I don't like saying it, but I reckon it *was* Liddy. Who else might have wanted to wind Jayne up?"

"Half the orchestra?" Pippa suggested with a faint grin.

Chris smothered a laugh. "Well, yeah, but not so much that they'd go to all that trouble. Liddy was the only one with a real motive. And it was easy for her, because she and Jayne are in the same room."

"You're starting to sound like a whodunnit," Pippa told him.

"Just call me Sherlock! Seriously, though, I think Liddy's out to get her own back on Jayne, and all this spooky whistling and stuff's down to her." He glanced around. "Where is she, anyway?"

Liddy wasn't with the main group ahead. Pippa looked back, but she wasn't behind them either. In fact, she reflected, she hadn't seen Liddy at all since they got to Low Aspen.

"You don't think she's up to something else, do you?" she asked uneasily.

"Could be." Chris frowned. "Look, Pippa, I

43

think one of us ought to talk to her. I mean, a joke's a joke, and Jayne did ask for it, but if she's planning to go on like this, well . . ."

"I know. It stops being funny after a while."

"Right. Liddy's made her point, so it's time to quit." He looked hopefully at her. "Would you . . .?"

Pippa shook her head. "You get on better with her than I do."

"Not really. Anyway, you're in the same room—"

"So's Jayne. Makes it harder."

"You've still got more chance than me of getting her on her own. Go on, Pippa, please. Give it a try."

Pippa didn't like the idea at all. Liddy would probably deny the whole thing, and they'd end up enemies. Even if they weren't exactly friends now, she didn't want that; and certainly not for Jayne's sake.

"I think we should wait a bit," she said. "I mean . . . nothing awful's happened, has it? Like you said, Liddy's made her point, so perhaps she *will* call it quits now."

Chris thought about that for a few moments, then nodded. "Maybe you're right. We could be completely wrong about her anyway, so . . ." He shrugged, and gave her a sheepish grin. "You're not the only one who's too gut-less to talk to her, so yeah, let's wait and see."

They walked on in silence. Pippa tried to concentrate on something else – the festival, for instance – but it wasn't easy. Something was bugging her, and she couldn't put a finger on it. Something she'd overlooked, or that didn't fit. What *was* it?

Without thinking, she glanced over her shoulder again. The hill dropped away behind her, and in the grey-green shade of the over-hanging tree tunnel she saw Liddy trailing along on her own. *Oh, well*, she thought. *At least she hasn't got herself lost.*

Then the thought froze and crumbled in her mind.

"Chris . . ." She grabbed his arm so hard that he jumped in surprise. "What's that?"

"What's what?" Chris looked back, too. "Oh, there's Liddy."

"Yeah." Pippa's heart had started to thump. "But what's that following her?"

"Huh?" Chris peered harder. "I can't see anything."

"There. About a couple of metres behind – see it? That shadow."

It was a small shadow, low to the ground, and it was gliding along the road in Liddy's wake. The shifting leaves above confused its shape – if it *had* a shape; she couldn't be sure – but there was no doubt in Pippa's mind that it was very definitely tracking Liddy.

"Hang on; I think it's—" Chris broke off as Liddy came out of the shade into sunlight. "No. Trick of the light. There's nothing there."

There wasn't, not now. But Pippa knew what she'd seen, and it hadn't been a trick. *Something* had been moving along the road at Liddy's heels. Something dark. Low to the ground. About the size of a smallish dog.

About the size of Lancer?

"Come on," Chris said. "If Liddy sees you staring like that, she'll get suspicious."

With a huge effort Pippa shook off the creeping fear that had got its claws into her. Liddy was in the full sun now, and the road behind her was empty. Whatever *it* was, it had vanished.

But Liddy was smiling. She hadn't noticed Pippa watching her, and the smile was for herself alone. A private smile.

And a very secret one.

When they got back to the Manor, there was some good news waiting for them. The last of the visiting orchestras had arrived that afternoon, and tonight the festival organisers were throwing a party to welcome everyone. There'd be food in the hall, then a disco.

"Just what we need before the really hard work starts!" Chris said, rubbing his hands together with anticipation. "Ready to dance till dawn, Pippa?"

"*I* am," declared Jayne, who'd got over her sulks and was pushing in again. "Come on, Pippa; let's go up to our room and decide what to wear." She towed Pippa off. Liddy was standing a few metres away, and as they passed her Jayne glanced slyly sideways. Pippa could see it coming; she just *knew* that Jayne wasn't going to be able to resist a bitchy remark. And she was right. Raising her voice, Jayne said: "You can come with us if you want, Liddy. But I don't suppose you've got any clothes worth deciding about."

"*Jayne!*" Pippa dug her with an elbow. "Cut it out, will you?"

"Why should I?" Jayne retorted. "After what she did to me."

She was on about the bone again. "You don't know it was her," said Pippa. "And even if it was, you asked for it. Just knock it off, before one of you does something *really* stupid."

Jayne just stuck her nose disdainfully in the

air and walked on. Pippa glanced back at Liddy. She was watching them, and her face had that sort of tight, closed look, as if someone had just slapped her.

Pippa's conscience twinged guiltily. Then Liddy caught her eye. She shrugged, and turned away before Pippa could say or do anything. But as she turned, Pippa thought she glimpsed a change in her expression. Faintly, privately, Liddy smiled.

Just as she'd smiled this afternoon, on the walk back from Low Aspen.

6

By the time the disco had been going for an hour or so, Pippa had completely forgotten about Liddy, Jayne or any other worries. She was having a brilliant time. The DJ played all her favourite music, and the hall was a seething mass of noise and light and jumping, gyrating dancers.

Liddy had turned up – she didn't really dance, just hung around the edge of the crowd and shuffled her feet a bit – but she seemed to have gone now. Jayne, of course, was in the thick of it, wearing a shiny Lycra outfit that must have cost a bomb, and showing off for all she was worth. She'd been a bit edgy while they were upstairs getting ready, looking over her shoulder every few minutes as though she'd heard something odd. But she seemed fine now, and as determined as ever to be the centre of attention.

Pippa was dancing with a boy from the French orchestra (he couldn't speak much English and she couldn't speak much French, but who cared?) when Jayne barged in and grabbed her arm, shouting something over the thump of the music.

"Can't hear you!" Pippa shouted back.

Jayne pulled her arm, dragging her off balance. The French boy grinned and shrugged, and Jayne tugged Pippa determinedly to the end of the hall, where the noise wasn't so loud.

"I want to go to the loo," she bawled in Pippa's ear. "Come with me!"

"*What?*" Pippa was astounded and furious. "You hauled me away because you want me to come to the *loo* with you? What's the matter with you? Go on your own!"

"My hair's coming undone!" Jayne shouted. "I can't fix it by myself. Oh, *please*, Pippa!"

Jayne had fixed her own hair perfectly well earlier, and Pippa was just about to say so – when she saw the look in Jayne's eyes. A haunted look. Jayne was trying to disguise it. But she was afraid of something.

"All right!" Pippa held her hands up as Jayne started to plead again. "Come on, then."

They slipped out of the hall. The nearest loos were at the back of the Manor, down some steps and along a basement corridor. Jayne almost ran, taking care to keep ahead of Pippa. As if she felt safer with someone behind her . . .

They barged through the door of the Ladies, then stopped. There was no one else in there, and under the cold fluorescent lights the row of half-open cubicle doors looked faintly menacing.

This is ridiculous! Pippa thought. *She* was getting the jitters now, catching them from Jayne. Of course there wasn't anything sinister here. It was just a loo!

"Go on, then, if you're going!" she said impatiently.

Jayne bit her lip. Then she strode to one of the cubicles, banging the door as wide open as it would go and peering round it before she went in. Pippa sighed, tapping her foot as she waited. She could hear Jayne humming, quite loudly, as if she was trying to bolster her confidence. *Crazy*, Pippa told herself. *Oh, hurry up, Jayne! Or I'll just leave you to—*

The thought fizzled out as she heard a noise from the passage outside.

It was only a small noise, but in her keyed-up state it shook Pippa. A sort of *scrape . . . click. Scrape . . . click*. And then something even stranger. Almost like a snuffle.

Somebody outside, with a cold, Pippa tried to convince herself. The door'd open any minute, and whoever it was would come in, and she'd feel a complete prat for being so jumpy.

But the door didn't open. And she could still hear the snuffling.

Then Jayne flushed the loo, and the snuffling was blotted out. On a sudden impulse, Pippa ran to the door and wrenched it open.

There was nothing in the passage. Nothing at all.

Mystified, and more than a bit uneasy, Pippa shut the door again. When she turned round, Jayne was at the washbasin, staring at her.

"What is it?" Jayne demanded. "What's the matter?"

"Nothing."

"There is!" Jayne's voice started to rise to a squeak. "Why were you looking out of the door?"

Pippa thought quickly. "I wasn't. I was getting fed up waiting, and I was going back to the disco."

"OK, OK, I'm coming!" Jayne washed her hands as if the world was going to end in three seconds, and rushed for the door without bothering to dry them. Pippa was equally glad to get out of there. *She* kept wanting to look over her shoulder now. And it wasn't just Jayne's nervousness infecting her.

They reached the entrance hall, and Pippa made a decision.

"You go back to the disco," she told Jayne. "I'm going upstairs for a minute."

Jayne didn't offer to come with her but hurried thankfully through the hall door. Pippa turned away towards the staircase, thinking hard. Liddy had disappeared from the hall a while ago. Pippa hadn't seen her since, and suddenly she very much wanted to know where she was. She'd check their room. Liddy might be there – but Pippa had a strong suspicion that she wasn't. In fact she'd have taken bets that, just a few minutes ago, Liddy had been down in the basement.

She could hear the muffled beat of the music as she climbed the stairs to the top floor. The upstairs lights were worked by push switches that only stayed on for about twenty seconds, just long enough to reach the next switch before the corridors were plunged into gloom again. It was a bit creepy to be walking along in bright light but with darkness before and behind her. Pippa hadn't minded it before, but now it felt different somehow. She almost wished she hadn't come on her own. Maybe if she went back, she could ask Chris . . .

Oh, grow up! she told herself. *You're not a kid.* Not far to go now; next left, then the room was only a few more steps, just past the bathroom.

She turned into the side passage and pressed yet another light switch. The bulb came on, showing a row of doors. Theirs was the third—

Pippa stopped, frowning. What was that, on the floor outside their door? It looked like a piece of crumpled paper, and she hurried to look more closely.

She reached the spot, bent to pick the object up . . . And stopped again. Because it wasn't a piece of paper.

It was another bone.

"What the—" Pippa whispered. This bone was a different shape to the first one: shorter and nearly triangular. Trying to remember biology lessons, Pippa thought it looked like a shoulder blade, though it was too small to be human.

Then, without any warning, the light went out.

Pippa jumped, and accidentally bit the inside of her cheek. It hurt, and with a hand to her face and mumbling swear words, she groped her way to the wall. There was another switch here somewhere – oh, where *was* it?

She was still fumbling and muttering, so she didn't hear the faint sound from behind her: the sound of a door opening, then closing again quickly and furtively. At last her fingers felt the switch and pressed it. Light flooded the corridor again, and Pippa turned to snatch up the bone.

It wasn't there.

"–*uh?*" Pippa stared with her mouth hanging idiotically open. Where had it *gone*? It had been right in front of her only ten seconds ago, and now it had vanished without trace!

She got down on her hands and knees, scrabbling, feeling the floorboards, as if she didn't believe what her eyes were telling her. The light went out again, she cursed it again, and while she was trying to find the switch a second time, their bedroom door opened.

"Pippa?" said Liddy. "What on earth are you doing?"

Pippa shot upright and spun round in a single movement. By the light coming from inside the room she saw that Liddy had changed the clothes she'd worn to the disco for jeans and a sweatshirt. So she certainly hadn't been in bed.

Liddy was still looking curious, and Pippa said, "I was trying to find the light switch." She did find it then, and whanged it on.

"Oh," said Liddy. "Right." A pause. "Did you come back for something?"

Pippa tried to think of an excuse, and came up with the obvious one. "I wondered if you were OK," she said. "Weren't you enjoying the disco?"

Liddy shook her head. "Not really."

There was another awkward silence, then suddenly Pippa blurted, "Look, Liddy, you mustn't let Jayne get to you! Everyone knows what she's like, and no one takes any notice of her."

Liddy looked down at her own feet. "Jayne's got nothing to do with it. I'm just not into discos. I'd rather practise my flute. That's why I came up here; I can play for a bit without anyone interrupting."

It was a clear hint that she wanted Pippa to go away. "Fine," Pippa said airily. "I'll leave you to get on with it, then. Oh, but there's just one thing."

"What?" Liddy asked cautiously.

Pippa looked her straight in the eye. "You wouldn't happen to have seen any more bones lying around, would you?"

Liddy was quick – but not quite quick enough. For one moment a flicker of guilt showed on her face before she worked it rapidly into an expression of surprise.

"Bones?" she repeated. "What on earth are you talking about? Of course I haven't seen any bones!"

"Right." Pippa nodded. "I thought you'd say that. See you, then."

Liddy stared at her for a moment or two, then shut the door.

The corridor light went out again. Pippa slammed it on once more and walked away down the passage, feeling grimly satisfied. She was sure she knew the truth now. The warfare was still going on, and it *had* been Liddy outside the loo, making those noises and trying to scare Jayne. Pippa had worked out where the bone had come from, too. There'd been roast lamb at dinner last night. Liddy must have raided the Manor dustbins, taken the bone and put it outside the door for Jayne to find. When she heard Pippa's voice, without Jayne, she'd quickly opened the door and snatched it back, then put on an act of puzzled innocence when Pippa tried to challenge her.

They're acting like a couple of kids, Pippa thought crossly. *Well, from now on they can get on with it. I'm not going to waste any more time on either of them!*

She could hear the disco again – one of the best albums ever. Pippa's scowl changed to a smile as she headed for the stairs. More dancing, that was what she needed. *She'd* show Jayne how it was done!

As she ran down the stairs, Pippa didn't see the figure that stood in the shadows on the landing above. Liddy watched until she was sure Pippa had gone back into the hall. Then she, too, hurried down the stairs, and ducked into a side passage that led to one of the outside doors.

Liddy was carrying her flute. There was something in her jeans pocket, too, making a slight, triangular bulge. Outside, it was fully dark now, and she flitted like a silent ghost to the sunken garden and down the brick steps. The pond glimmered. The statues glimmered too, looking pale and unnervingly real in the starlight. Liddy went to the statue of Lancer, and laid her hand on his stone head.

"You're a good dog, Lancer," she whispered softly. "And *you* like my playing, don't you?" She smiled, and thrust her hand into her pocket. "I'll just hide this with the others, and then I'll play for you again, shall I? That's right. I'll play for you."

She moved deeper into the long grass and was gone for maybe a minute. Then she returned, sat down in the grass next to the statue, and slowly, dreamily, lifted the flute to her lips.

7

Jayne had more bad dreams that night.

Pippa was so tired that she thought nothing could wake her up; but Jayne did. She was tossing and turning as she'd done before, and calling out, "Go away, go *away*!" Again, Pippa couldn't shake her out of it. And again the nightmares stopped as suddenly as they'd begun, so that one moment Jayne was struggling and whimpering, and the next she was sleeping peacefully.

Baffled, Pippa stepped back. She turned round – and saw the silhouette of Liddy sitting up in bed.

"Is she having more dreams?" Liddy asked softly.

Pippa was surprised. She'd been too busy trying to wake Jayne to give Liddy a thought, but now the fact that she was here took her aback. Somehow, she'd expected her to be missing again.

"Yeah," she said aloud. "They've stopped now. But it was just like last night – I couldn't wake her up."

There was a lamp between Pippa and Liddy's beds, and Liddy switched it on. "She looks all right," she said, peering.

"I know," Pippa replied. "If it's like last night, she'll just sleep through now. We might as well get back to sleep too, if we can."

Liddy sighed. "I was having a *lovely* dream. And she's gone and spoiled it."

"Well, the day Jayne stops being selfish, you can call me Queen Victoria." Pippa couldn't resist the barb, but Liddy didn't even smile. "Come on, turn the light off. I'm *tired*."

Despite her tiredness, though, Pippa found it hard to go back to sleep. She could hear Jayne and Liddy breathing on either side of her, and she felt like piggy-in-the-middle. Stuck between two enemies and trying to keep the peace. Some chance!

At least the second bone hadn't been put under Jayne's bed. Pippa had checked, fishing with a rolled-up magazine, but all she'd found was a grubby sock and a load of fluff. She didn't know what Liddy had done with it, but right now she didn't care. If Liddy hadn't pulled that stunt again tonight, perhaps peace *would* reign for a while.

All the same, a question was nagging at Pippa. She didn't understand why Jayne should be having these nightmares. It was easy to blame the bone, of course. But – despite her rude remark to Pippa – when it came to being thick-skinned, Jayne took the biscuit. It wasn't like her to be freaked. Then there were the nervy bouts, such as the incident in the loo. Something was scaring Jayne. Something more than just the bone. And Pippa couldn't work out what it was.

Maybe she should talk to Chris again. Maybe between them they could find out what was really bugging Jayne, then tackle Liddy – not chicken out this time but *really* do it.

Or maybe . . .

She didn't know why she had the thought, and she certainly didn't like it. But it came creeping up on her, squatted in her brain and refused to be budged. It said: *Or maybe we should take another look at that statue?*

Pippa shivered under the duvet, and with a

great effort pushed the thought away. *Stop being so stupid*, she told herself. *Think about something else, then make yourself go to sleep. Go on, you can do it.*

She did, eventually. Outside, a light wind blew through the garden, and a trail of cloud drifted across the moon. All the shadows faded and merged with the dark.

Or *almost* all the shadows.

No one was awake to see the small silhouette that moved low to the ground, gliding along the outside of the house. No one was awake to see it turn in at a side door. Or, a few minutes later, to hear the faint sounds; a snuffling, and a rhythmic *scrape . . . click. Scrape . . . click.* No one knew when the sounds stopped.

Outside the door of the three girls' room.

Then there was another noise. A faint *thud*. As if something small and hard had been dropped on the floor. Very deliberately. Very carefully.

Like a faithful dog bringing home a special prize . . .

In the morning, Pippa expected Jayne to be in a filthy temper. But she wasn't. In fact, she was very subdued, hardly saying a word as they got ready to go downstairs for breakfast.

Liddy was up and about earlier than anyone, and had already been out in the garden when Pippa finished dressing. She came back looking bright-eyed and a bit excited, but she didn't say anything to either of them. Jayne glared at her, but she stayed quiet, too, and that in itself made Pippa uneasy. She'd never seen Jayne like this. Normally she was loud, brash, always ready to argue. This morning, though, she wouldn't have said "boo" to a goose.

And she still kept looking nervously over her shoulder.

None of them ate much breakfast. Pippa was tired, Liddy seemed to be off in a dream world of her own, and Jayne just sat staring at her plate as if she'd found worms on it instead of toast and marmalade.

Or bones.

At last Pippa couldn't stand it any longer. Liddy was far enough away down the table not to overhear, so she decided to plunge in.

"Jayne," she said.

Jayne visibly started, then turned and gave her a furious look.

"Don't make me jump like that!" she snapped.

"I didn't; I only said 'Jayne'."

"Oh. Well, what, then?"

"I just wondered . . . are you OK? You seem a bit—"

"I'm fine," Jayne interrupted before Pippa could find the right word. "I slept badly, that's all." She paused. "I had a *horrible* dream."

"What about?" asked Pippa.

Jayne shuddered. "I don't want to talk about it. *Ever*."

Pippa shrugged and drank her tea. All right, she'd tried. If Jayne didn't want to open up, she wasn't going to push it.

Neither of them said anything else for a while – until Jayne unexpectedly broke the silence.

"It was chasing me," she said, in a peculiar, clipped little voice. "Following. Everywhere I went."

"What was?" Pippa asked, baffled.

Jayne turned to look at her. Her lower lip was trembling, as if she was about to cry.

"In my dream," she said. "I couldn't shake it off, Pippa. Whatever I did, however hard I tried, it was always *there*."

She seemed to have forgotten that she "didn't want to talk about it, ever" because suddenly, in a rush, the whole story was blurted out. In her nightmare, Jayne had found herself being steadily and determinedly pursued by something. She didn't know what it was, because she never saw it. But she heard it breathing, and she heard it padding along behind her. It never grew tired, it never gave up. And it never actually *did* anything. But it was always there.

And it terrified Jayne half out of her mind.

"I can't stand it," she said dramatically. "I just *can't*! If it happens again, I'll go completely crazy!" Abruptly she grabbed Pippa's arm. "I don't want to sleep tonight! Sit up with me, Pippa, and help me stay awake!"

"All night?" Pippa said. "You've got to be kidding! I need my sleep, even if you don't!"

"Please!" Jayne begged. "It's easier with two; if I do it on my own, I'm scared I'll fall asleep. *Please*, Pippa, you've got to!"

Pippa didn't think she'd "got to" anything where Jayne was concerned. She certainly didn't owe her any favours! But two things stopped her from saying so. Firstly, Jayne *was* genuinely frightened, and Pippa wouldn't wish that on anyone. And secondly, if she stayed awake tonight, it was just possible that she might discover the answers to a few questions.

"All right, then," she said. "But just this once. And if *I* fall asleep, don't blame me!" She paused. "What about Liddy? We could ask her if—"

"No!" Jayne said quickly and so vehemently. "I don't want her involved. I don't even want her to *know*!"

"OK, OK, calm down! She'll have to know *something*. If she sees us sitting up all night, she'll ask questions."

"Then she mustn't see," said Jayne firmly. "Till she goes to sleep, we'll pretend we're sleeping, too. Then we can find things to do that don't make any noise. There's some board games in the common-room here; we can get those and play them."

"All right. You sort that out." Pippa looked up and realized suddenly that they were almost the only people left in the hall. "Hey, everyone else has finished. We're going to be late for rehearsal!"

"How am I supposed to think about rehearsal when all *this* is going on?" Jayne complained.

"Because the festival starts tomorrow, and if you *don't* think about it, Mr Elwood'll go completely ballistic," Pippa told her. "That's *much* worse than nightmares!"

Jayne groaned theatrically, but she got up all the same and headed for the door, leaving

Pippa to take both their plates back to the counter. Pippa scowled at her disappearing back, then sighed. Tonight might prove to be *extremely* interesting.

Or the most boring and tedious night she'd ever spent in her life.

8

Some people, Pippa thought, never learned. OK, so Jayne was strung-out and maybe that explained some of it. But it wasn't really an excuse. The simple fact was that, in the rehearsal hall, Jayne couldn't stop herself from having a go at Liddy whenever she got the chance.

It was only a couple of small things this time. A snide remark or two, meant to be overheard; then when Liddy's back was turned, Pippa saw Jayne swop over two pages of her music, so that she couldn't find her cue and the practice ground to a halt. Mr Elwood was *not* pleased. Liddy, as usual, took the tongue-lashing he gave her in humiliated silence, while Jayne just sat with a patient, superior and pitying expression on her face. Pippa almost changed her mind about the promise she'd made. But then she reminded herself that she was doing it for her own reasons rather than Jayne's.

She'd hoped to talk to Chris after rehearsal finished, but before she could find him, Jayne latched on to her.

"Let's go in to the town this afternoon," she said.

"I'm busy," Pippa replied tersely.

"But I don't want to go on my own!" Jayne protested.

"Well, you should have come with the rest of us yesterday, shouldn't you? Anyway, we've got more practice this afternoon, then Mr Elwood wants us all for a meeting, so there won't be enough time."

Jayne's mouth set into a sulky pout. "I don't care if I miss the meeting. It's only going to be about—"

She stopped, and looked quickly over her shoulder.

Before she could even think about it, Pippa looked too. There was no one behind them, nothing there at all. But Jayne had turned dead-white.

"What's the matter?" Pippa asked.

"N-nothing." Jayne sounded nervous. "I just thought . . ."

"What?"

But Jayne shook her head. "Doesn't matter." She paused. "Don't forget what you promised! About tonight."

"I'm hardly likely to, am I, with you nagging me about it every two minutes!" Pippa retorted grumpily. She could see Chris in the distance; he was with a group of other boys. Damn. She'd hoped to get him on his own, but it looked like they were all going off together.

Suddenly she felt thoroughly fed up with Jayne. OK, she'd keep her promise about tonight. But until then she didn't want to be around Jayne any more.

Saying, "I've got things to do. See you later," she turned and walked away. She heard Jayne call after her, but ignored it. Let her stew. Pippa was going to get something to eat, then find a quiet, sunny spot in the garden where no one would disturb her.

Pippa could walk fast when she wanted to, and once she was well clear she turned to make sure Jayne wasn't following. To her relief, she saw Jayne trailing up the stairs. She was about half way up –

Then she seemed to freeze in mid-step.

Pippa frowned. Even from here she could see that Jayne's hand had gripped the banister rail with sudden intensity. Then, slowly, Jayne turned her head. She didn't notice Pippa. She was looking back down the stairs, and her expression was one of stark fear. It only lasted for a moment or two before it changed to a frown; then the tension seemed to slide away from Jayne and she carried on walking up the stairs.

She hadn't seen anything.

But Pippa had.

Or thought she had. Because it was really only a shadow. But it had been an odd shape, small and low. And it had seemed to move with a life of its own, flowing up the stairs on Jayne's heels. When Jayne had stopped, it had stopped.

And when Jayne looked back, it suddenly wasn't there any more.

Pippa remembered what she and Chris had seen yesterday: Liddy, walking up the hill from Low Aspen, with a small, dark shape trailing her. A shape that vanished as soon as she emerged into the sunshine.

Just a trick of the light, they'd told themselves at the time.

Now, Pippa wasn't quite so sure.

That afternoon, it was Pippa's turn to get on the wrong side of Mr Elwood. However hard she tried, she couldn't concentrate on the rehearsal. Her mind was buzzing with too many other problems. Jayne was in as bad a state, and at last Mr Elwood declared exasperatedly: "In all my years of teaching and conducting, I've never met such a sorry shower! Liddy this morning, now Pippa and Jayne. Wake up, the lot of you! All right, we'll leave this piece for now and see if we can manage 'English Country Garden' without *totally* wrecking that! Find your music." He waited, tapping his baton impatiently. "Ready? Then on the count of – oh, for heaven's sake, Jayne, what's the matter *now*?"

Jayne was scrabbling in her bag. "My music's gone! It isn't here!"

Mr Elwood sighed. "Then you must have left it behind, mustn't you?"

"I didn't!" Jayne wailed. She had tipped her bag upside-down and was rummaging through papers scattered all over the floor. "It was in here this morning, I saw it!"

"Did you really?" said Mr Elwood with heavy sarcasm. "Well, well. The Gremlins of Aspen

Manor must have spirited it away when you weren't looking, mustn't they? I mean, you'd never be so careless as to *lose* it!"

Jayne started to protest again, but a glare silenced her. "I'm not going to waste any more time, Jayne," Mr Elwood said sternly. "Share with Pippa. And now, may we get *on*?"

Jayne all but shoved Pippa off her chair as she moved closer to share music stands, and Pippa grinned. She wouldn't mind betting she knew where Jayne's music had gone. Liddy, of course. She'd probably hidden it somewhere. Oh, well – it was a better way of paying her back than bones.

"What are you smirking at?" Jayne hissed.

"Me?" said Pippa innocently. "Nothing at all."

She tucked her violin under her chin and resisted the urge to giggle as she raised her bow.

By the time everyone went to bed, Pippa was regretting the promise she'd made to Jayne. After last night's disco, and what had happened afterwards, she felt so tired that she could cheerfully have gone to sleep standing on her head. The idea of forcing herself to stay awake just so Jayne didn't get scared seemed deeply stupid. In fact, she thought, Jayne had conned her.

To make matters worse, Liddy wasn't in any hurry to go to bed tonight. She took ages undressing, then sat around in her pyjamas, taking her flute to pieces and cleaning it. Jayne glared daggers at her and made loud remarks about turning the light off, but Liddy took no notice. Pippa just lay down and stared at the ceiling. She didn't want to get involved.

At last, though, Liddy got into bed and switched off the lamp. As the room plunged into darkness Jayne leaned across to Pippa and whispered in her ear: "Give her half an hour. That should be long enough."

"Shh! She'll hear you," Pippa muttered back. "Anyway, how am I supposed to know how long half an hour is? I can't see my watch in the dark."

"Count it, or something."

"*You* count it. This was your idea."

Jayne snorted, and Pippa heard her mattress springs creak as she turned her back. For some time there was silence. The moon showed vaguely through the curtains, and Pippa watched it, wondering how fast it moved and whether she could work out the time by how far it travelled across the window. She yawned.

This was boring. If she wasn't careful she'd fall asleep anyway. Well, so what? It would just be Jayne's bad luck, wouldn't it?

As she thought that, someone started to snore. The noise was coming from Jayne's bed, and she raised her eyebrows. *She accuses ME of snoring?* she thought. *Well, let her get on with it. It's not my fault if she can't stay awake!*

She was about to sit up and double-check that Jayne really was sleeping. But someone else beat her to it. Pippa heard the sound of Liddy's feet on the floor just in time, and she froze, peering out from under the duvet. She saw Liddy's silhouette appear from behind her, saw her tiptoe to Jayne's bed and stand for a few moments looking down. Then she turned towards Pippa. Pippa shut her eyes and lay as still as a statue, trying to breathe naturally. She must have fooled Liddy, because after a few more seconds she heard her pad away again. Other noises followed: small shufflings and rustlings. Pippa didn't dare look, but it sounded as if Liddy was putting some clothes on.

Then she heard the feet again. Or rather, shoes; the soles squeaked slightly on the floorboards. A *click* – that was the door opening. Then a faint *tap* as it closed again.

Pippa shot upright in bed. It took her less than three seconds to be sure that Liddy had gone. And she'd taken her flute with her.

What to do? Pippa looked at Jayne. She was sound asleep, all right. Should she wake her and tell her what was going on? No. Jayne would be more trouble than she was worth. If Pippa wanted to find out what Liddy was up to, the only way was to follow her. Alone.

She threw on a sweatshirt and leggings and shoved her feet into her trainers. She wished she had a torch, but she didn't – anyway, she wouldn't have dared use it, in case she gave herself away. Hurrying to the door, she opened it and peeked out into the corridor. No sign of Liddy. Which way was she most likely to have gone? To the main stairs, probably. Down to the front door.

Sneaking through the corridors (which were unnervingly dark, though she tried not to think too hard about that) Pippa suddenly heard someone moving ahead of her. She slowed down and stopped at a turn in the passage, flattening herself against the wall before peering cautiously round.

Liddy, wearing a jumper over her old-fashioned pyjamas, was on the stairs, heading for the ground floor. Moonlight made strange patterns in the huge entrance hall, and for a moment it looked to Pippa as if the shadows down there were closing in to meet Liddy as she hurried towards them. Wide-eyed, she watched as Liddy reached the bottom of the stairs and became a shadow herself. She didn't go towards the front door, though. Instead, she turned aside and disappeared through one of the arches that led to the back of the house.

Pippa hesitated. She desperately wanted to know where Liddy was going, but she had to admit that she was more than a little scared. The prospect of being alone in the dark maze of the house, at dead of night, was *not* pleasant. What if she got lost, and couldn't find her way back?

Don't be so gutless! another part of her said. This wasn't Nathaniel Thornbury's Victorian age. If she did get lost, or really frightened, all she had to do was switch some lights on. *Come on, Pippa,* she urged herself, *or you're never going to find out the truth!*

Taking a deep breath, she ran towards the staircase.

9

Liddy was out of sight by the time Pippa reached the arch. But her soft, quick footsteps were still audible, and Pippa followed the sound, moving very cautiously now. After a while the footsteps stopped; then came a click and a grating creak. A door being opened? Pippa crept forward. Then a dim grey light appeared ahead. Moonlight. So Liddy *was* going outside after all, but through a side door.

Pippa waited until she was sure Liddy was well clear of the house, then ran towards the faint light. She'd lost her sense of direction and couldn't work out where she would emerge. But when she saw the door, and what was beyond it, everything dropped into place.

Liddy had gone to the sunken garden. Pippa could see her in the moonlight, hurrying down the brick steps. She was heading – of course – for the statues.

But what was she going to *do* there?

Curiosity overcame Pippa's nerves. Hunching down, so that if Liddy looked back she wouldn't see her against the skyline, she scurried like an animal to the top of the steps, and ducked behind one of the square pillars that flanked them. When she peeked round the edge of the pillar, Liddy had reached the statues and was crouching down beside the figure of Lancer. She started to stroke the stone dog's head and Pippa's mouth opened in a silent "O" of shock.

For it seemed that, very slowly and very stiffly, Lancer's head was *moving*.

She gripped the pillar, staring in disbelief. It was her imagination, it *had* to be! Statues didn't move, they wouldn't, they *couldn't* . . .

Then Liddy stepped back – and Pippa realized her mistake. Lancer wasn't moving. Liddy's shadow, cast by the moon, had fallen across the statue, and for a moment it had created the illusion that it was alive. Pippa felt relieved, shaken and completely stupid all at once. But what was Liddy doing now? She'd moved away from the statue and was peering around, as if she was searching for something.

Or waiting? Pippa tensed again. If only she could get closer, and see properly what was going on! Those bushes on the far side of the sunken garden would give her good cover. But could she reach them without alerting Liddy?

Cautiously, Pippa backed away from the pillar. She was pretty sure that Liddy wouldn't look up. If she made a wide circle and approached the bushes from behind, she should be able to get a much better view.

As she started to circle round, the soft trill of a flute drifted up from the sunken garden. Pippa knew it must be Liddy, but all the same the sound made her shiver. In the quiet emptiness of night it was eerie and lonely, as if a ghost was playing.

Don't get scared, she told herself. *It IS only Liddy; you'll see for yourself in a minute.* The bushes were ahead of her now. They looked very dense and dark, and for a moment she almost lost her nerve at the thought of creeping in among them.

Come on, Pippa! With a determined effort Pippa scuttled the last few metres, and slid in among the shrubs. Branches scratched her face and the leaves were thicker than she'd expected, but she pushed her way forward, trying not to make any noise, until, parting the last layer of twigs, she could see the garden again.

Liddy stood in the long grass, with her flute to her lips. She wasn't playing a tune as such; it was more like a series of trilling whistles. Rising and falling. Rising and falling. Pippa found herself almost hypnotized.

Until she saw what was coming through the long grass behind Liddy's figure.

The shadow was small and dark, and it moved with a weird, shuffling-gliding motion. Pippa had seen it before. Twice.

Only this time, she *knew* she wasn't imagining it.

Waves of heat and cold chased each other over Pippa's skin as she stared at the slowly moving shadow. It had no face, no features at all; its shape was completely and blankly black. But there could be no doubt of what it was. A dog. The size and shape of Lancer.

The shadow was almost at Liddy's heels now, and Pippa wanted to yell, "Look out, look behind you!" But before she could do anything, Liddy turned. She saw the shape. She stopped playing. She *smiled*.

And Pippa heard her voice.

"Good boy, Lancer. *Good* boy."

There was something in the shadow's mouth – or where its mouth should have been. Pippa couldn't make it out, but it seemed to be a small, pale object, about the size of her own hand. The shadow shambled right to Liddy's feet, and Liddy crouched down, reaching towards it. Pippa saw her take the small object, then she spoke again.

"That's another one . . . Good boy, Lancer – you're a *faithful* dog."

Despite the fear churning inside her, Pippa was horribly fascinated. What did this *mean?* What was the object the shadow had given to Liddy? Could ghosts carry solid things? Or wasn't it a ghost at all? Could it possibly be a real, living animal?

Liddy straightened up, and turned to face the Manor. The silhouette at her feet tensed. Then Liddy raised one hand and pointed at the house. The shadow-dog's ears pricked, and, as if obeying a command, it moved away from her. Pippa shivered as she saw that it didn't trot or run like an ordinary animal, but instead seemed to glide, as if its paws weren't quite touching the ground. Its shape flickered along the edge of the pond, heading towards the brick steps. Liddy stood watching it go. She was still holding her flute, but she wasn't interested in playing it now. She was smiling. She looked *pleased*.

Then, so fast that Pippa was completely unprepared for it, a cloud covered the moon. Pippa yelped with shock as the entire scene plunged into darkness, and suddenly her fear exploded into something far more powerful. She couldn't see anything! The dark was like a suffocating blanket, closing in on her, trapping her. Panicking, she flailed her arms, trying to break free of the bushes, struggling to stop herself from screaming. . .

And the cloud cleared.

The moonlight seemed stunningly bright after the awful darkness, and Pippa froze, blinking and shuddering as the dizzy terror lost its grip. Sense came back, and she thought in alarm: *Did Liddy hear me? Have I given myself away?*

Quickly, she parted the bushes and looked down into the sunken garden.

Liddy had vanished.

And so had the shadow-dog.

Pippa's heart started to beat painfully fast again. Liddy must have heard her when she panicked, and she'd run away. Where had she gone? Back to the Manor, or was she still in the garden somewhere?

And what about the dog?

Very, very carefully, Pippa pulled the branches further apart and poked her head out. Now, she could see quite a long way beyond the sunken garden, but there was still no sign of anything moving. No Liddy. No small silhouette gliding towards the house. They'd both disappeared without trace.

Pippa took several deep breaths, trying to calm her nerves and think sensibly. Liddy couldn't have gone far in the short time that the moon had been behind the cloud. She must still be in the sunken garden, hiding, probably, in the long grass behind the statues. The dog, though . . . Who knew how fast it could move? It could be anywhere. In the house? On the far side of the grounds?

Or lurking only a few paces away . . .?

Suddenly, Pippa wanted to get out of the garden. She wanted it very badly. Groping and pushing, trying not to let panic rise again, she forced her way out of the shrubbery and emerged, breathless, into the open. Nervously she looked towards the Manor. She couldn't *see* anything between her and the safety of the door. And she was a fairly fast runner. It would take less than half a minute to cover that distance. Just let her get her breath back, and then –

Behind her, something rustled.

Pippa's legs locked solid under her, as if her feet were rooted into the ground. Slowly, fearfully, she started to turn her head.

An indistinct shape was prowling round the far side of the shrubbery. She could see its shadow in the moonlight, right at the edge of the bushes. It paused, and there was another rustling sound, as if it was pushing the branches apart, searching for her.

Then, she heard the unmistakable *huff* of someone – or something – breathing.

Terror smashed into Pippa's mind and she flung herself forward and pelted over the grass, running as she'd never run before. The house was ahead – she had to reach it, *had* to – *Oh, no; don't let it chase me, don't let it come after me, don't, don't, DON'T* –

If she'd turned her head, she might have seen Liddy emerge from behind the bushes and stare across the grass at her running figure. But Pippa was far too frightened to look back. With a choking cry she reached the side door and threw herself at it, scrabbling for the handle. The door juddered open; she stumbled through, spun round and slammed it behind her with a crash that echoed through the building. Then she took off down the passage, racing, not knowing or caring where she ended up, until suddenly she rushed out into the entrance hall.

Pippa sagged to her knees on the hall floor, feeling as if her lungs were going to burst. The moon was shining in at the main window now, flooding the hall with cold, dim light. But she was too winded to notice the small, dark patch of shadow that was moving on the far side. The patch of shadow that glided up the stairs and faded into the gloom of the top floor.

After a minute Pippa got to her feet and tottered towards the staircase. The worst of the panic was gone, but she felt sick and giddy and as weak as a small kitten. She just wanted to get to her room, huddle under the duvet and hide.

She reached the top of the stairs and thankfully pressed the landing light switch. The light sprang to brilliant life –

And at the same instant, from the direction of her bedroom, a shriek of sheer terror echoed through the Manor like a banshee-wail.

10

"Help me! Oh, somebody, *help meee*!"

Charging along the corridor, Pippa cannoned into Ms Lane, the music teacher, who came running from her own room.

"What on earth—" Ms Lane began in alarm.

"It's Jayne!" Pippa didn't know how she could be certain, but she was. And she was right. As she and Ms Lane raced round the corner and Ms Lane slammed the next corridor light on, they saw Jayne in the open doorway of the girls' bedroom. She was clutching the door frame, her eyes shut tightly and her face twisted in terror.

"Jayne!" Ms Lane ran to her, grabbing her

88

arms. "What is it? What's happened?"

Three other people appeared, hurrying towards them, and Pippa heard more footsteps in the distance.

"Oh, Ms Lane!" Jayne's eyes opened as wide as an owl's. "It was so *horrible*!" She burst into noisy sobs.

Everyone crowded round, all asking questions at once, until Ms Lane snarled at them to "Shut *up*!"

"What was horrible, Jayne?" she cajoled. "What was it?"

"I could *hear* it!" Jayne wailed. "Snuffling and scratching and – and *breathing*! It was by my *bed*, it was *there*, it was – oh, oh, oh!"

There wasn't much point in trying to get any sense out of her, so Ms Lane tried to shepherd her back into the bedroom. But Jayne only started to yell again.

"It might still be in there! I'm not going back in, I'm not, I'm *not*!"

Mr Elwood, in his dressing-gown, appeared at that moment. "What the blazes is going on?" he demanded.

"Jayne's had a bad fright," said Ms Lane. "She seems to think there's something horrible in her room, and she won't go back inside."

Mr Elwood sighed. "Festival nerves, I expect.

89

All right; take her for some hot, sweet tea or something, and I'll check the room to make sure."

As Ms Lane led the shivering Jayne away, Mr Elwood noticed Pippa.

"You share with Jayne, don't you?" he said. "What happened?"

"I don't know, Mr Elwood," Pippa replied innocently. "I woke up and went to the loo, and I was in there when Jayne started screaming." She paused. "I expect she had a bad dream."

"Yes, probably. Where's the third girl – Liddy, isn't it?"

"She's – er – she went for a drink of water," Pippa improvised. "We were both awake, and she was feeling a bit sick."

He rolled his eyes heavenwards. "Good grief, you're all like cats on hot bricks! Oh well, it can't be helped. Let's check your room, then perhaps some of us can get some sleep!"

He went into the bedroom, switching the light on. As Pippa followed, someone else slipped through the door with her. It was Chris, who said loudly, "I'll help, shall I?"

"Yes, yes, all right." Mr Elwood wasn't really listening. He was standing in the middle of the floor, staring around. "Can you see anything strange, Pippa?"

"No," said Pippa. "It looks just the same as usual." Then she sniffed and frowned. "Except—"

The words cut off in a stifled yelp as Chris trod, hard, on her foot. Pippa turned on him, but stopped as he put a finger to his mouth. There was a very intense look on his face. He'd noticed what she had, Pippa realized, but Mr Elwood hadn't. And Chris was warning her to play dumb.

The room might look the same as usual – but it didn't *smell* the same. There was a strange, heavy odour in the air; a sort of earth smell, dank and musty. Like a damp cellar that hadn't been opened for years. Or like something else. Something she recognized. What? She couldn't quite place it.

Mr Elwood opened the wardrobe, but nothing jumped out at him. Then he looked under the beds. First Liddy's, then Pippa's.

"I'll look at this one, Mr Elwood," said Chris, sounding helpful and dropping to his knees by Jayne's bed before Mr Elwood could reach it. He peered. "Nothing there."

But Pippa had seen him reach out and grab something.

"All right," said Mr Elwood wearily. "There's nothing funny going on. Jayne was just having a nightmare. Back to bed, everyone. That means you, too, Chris."

Chris had been about to show Pippa what he'd found, but there was no chance now. As he headed for the door he whispered to her, "*Sunken garden – six o'clock, before the others are up!*"

Pippa nodded. Then, as Chris and Mr Elwood went out, Liddy appeared.

"Ah, Liddy. Feeling better?" asked Mr Elwood.

Liddy looked blank, and Pippa rushed in quickly. "Jayne had a bad dream and started screaming. You must have been downstairs getting your drink of water, or you'd have heard her."

"Oh . . ." said Liddy, quickly hiding her flute behind her back. "Um . . . yes."

"Not feeling sick now?" Mr Elwood persisted.

"Sick? Oh – oh, no, I'm fine. Thanks." She gave Pippa a look that clearly said, *What are you up to?* but Pippa looked away. She didn't quite know why she'd covered up for Liddy. It was an impulse, and now it seemed pretty stupid. But if she was going to find out the truth – the *real* truth – she had a strong feeling that involving the teachers would cause more problems than it solved.

Everyone said goodnight, and Pippa and Liddy shut the door. Jayne wouldn't be back tonight, Pippa knew. Which meant she and Liddy would be alone. And she wanted some answers.

"OK," Pippa said, sitting down on her own bed. "So where were you really?"

Liddy looked wary. "Downstairs."

"Getting a drink of water? Like I told Mr Elwood?"

"Yes." Liddy turned her head away.

"And you didn't go outside?"

"No, of course I didn't! Look, I'm tired. I'm going to turn the light off, then I want to go to sleep." Liddy pressed the switch and the room sank into darkness. Pippa saw her shadowy figure cross the floor, then she got into bed and mumbled, " 'Night."

Pippa didn't answer. Instead she sat looking at the silhouette of Liddy's bed. Well, she'd found out one thing, at least. If Liddy *had* heard someone else in the garden, she didn't know it was Pippa. That was useful, because it meant she wouldn't be suspicious.

But it didn't answer any of Pippa's questions. Alarming questions. *Frightening* questions.

And it didn't do anything to stop the awful

certainty she felt, that this mystery was turning nasty . . . and dangerous.

She got under her duvet and lay down. Six o'clock, Chris had whispered. No need to set her alarm. She wasn't going to sleep tonight. No way.

No way.

By half-past five Pippa was up and dressing in the pearly light of dawn. Liddy slept on peacefully. Once she sighed and muttered, but she didn't wake, and Pippa tiptoed out of the room and hurried downstairs. Half an hour before Chris would turn up. She didn't want to go to the garden; it wasn't properly light yet, and the thought of waiting there on her own was a bit too spooky for comfort.

Or should she? Wasn't she just being a complete chicken? After all, it was the perfect chance to have a good look round for any clues. And the daylight was getting stronger every minute.

Come on, Pippa, she told herself firmly. *Get a grip. Whatever was out there last night, it won't still be hanging around, will it?* No, it wouldn't be. Because the memory of Jayne's wailing, terrified voice was sharp in her mind.

"Snuffling and scratching and breathing . . . It was by my bed . . ."

Oh, yes, Pippa had a good idea of where the shadow-dog had gone last night. A *very* good idea.

Clenching her teeth without realizing she was doing it, she opened the front door and headed for the sunken garden.

Chris arrived ten minutes later. Pippa was relieved to see him. She hadn't found any clues, and even though the sun was now rising, the atmosphere in the sunken garden was starting to give her the creeps. It was so quiet there that even the slightest noise made her jump like a scared rabbit. When, once, some small creature – probably a mouse – had scuttled through the long grass a few metres away, she'd almost turned tail and pelted back to the Manor.

"You're early," said Chris as he came down the steps.

"So are you." Pippa tried to sound casual but it didn't really work.

"Yeah, well, I didn't sleep much . . . Look, let's go over there. Away from the statues."

So he was spooked, too. Pippa followed him

back to the top end of the garden. Chris had a plastic carrier bag in his hand, and when they reached the steps he said, "I've brought what I found last night. Take a look at this."

He pulled a tatty sheet of paper out of the bag. Pippa stared at it blankly for a few moments before she realized what it was.

"Jayne's music! The piece she couldn't find yesterday!" She grabbed it from him. "Oh, yuk, it's all soggy!"

"Yeah," said Chris. "And shredded. Like something's been chewing it."

Noises by Jayne's bed, scratching and snuffling . . . A cold, liquid feeling clutched at Pippa's stomach, and she looked up at Chris, aghast.

"You heard what Jayne said. What scared her—"

"Yeah." Chris's face was grim. "But that isn't the only thing I found."

There was a moment's silence. Then Pippa said, in a very small voice: "What else?"

"These." Chris pulled them out. A pair of tights. Bright blue. Neither Pippa nor Liddy had tights that colour, so they could only be Jayne's. In fact Jayne had been wearing them yesterday evening, Pippa remembered. She'd seen her take them off and put them away in her drawer.

But something had taken them out again.

Taken them out, and torn them to shreds.

11

Pippa told Chris the whole story. Everything that had happened, everything she knew, and the things she didn't know but could only guess at. She wasn't sure if he'd believe all of it, especially the bit about the shadow-dog; when she'd glimpsed it in Low Aspen, he'd thought it was just a trick of the light. But Chris didn't laugh. He just listened, without interrupting her once.

When she finished, he had something to tell her.

"I've seen that shadow, too," he said sombrely. "Three times."

"You *have*?" Pippa stared at him, feeling

excited, relieved and horrified all at once. "When?"

The first time, she learned, was two nights ago, when Chris thought he'd glimpsed something small and dark and low to the ground scurrying across the entrance hall as he came downstairs for the disco. The second time had been yesterday evening, while they were all having dinner in the refectory. And the third . . .

"It was last night," he said. "Something woke me up, and I was trying to get back to sleep when I heard a weird noise outside my room. Sort of scuffling or scratching. So I went to have a look. I put the passage light on, and I was just in time to see that shadow disappearing round a corner. I *knew* I hadn't imagined it then. And a few minutes later, Jayne started screaming." He paused. "Jayne's the link, Pippa. The first time I saw it, I bumped into Jayne half a minute afterwards. The second time, she was in the disco, right by the door. And the third time . . . well, you know what happened."

Pippa nodded, mentally adding a few more items to the list. The bones. The noises she'd heard outside the loo. Now, the chewed-up music and the ruined tights. Chris was right –

every time, it all came back to Jayne.

The shadow-dog was following Jayne around. Tracking her. Haunting her.

Threatening her . . .?

Pippa swallowed, and said very softly: "*Faithful beyond death . . .*"

"You think it's Lancer." It was a statement, not a question.

Pippa nodded again. "Yeah." She hesitated, wondering if she dared say the rest. Then thought: *I've got to.* "And I think Liddy's using him. To get Jayne."

From the long silence she knew that Chris had been thinking exactly the same thing. They both stared around the garden, which seemed completely pleasant and harmless in the bright new daylight. Even the statues had an innocent look this morning.

At last, Chris spoke. His voice was just a little bit unsteady.

"Three questions," he said. "One: how the hell has she done it? Two: how are we going to stop it? And three: what's going to happen if we can't?"

Pippa couldn't even begin to come up with an answer to the first question. She didn't want to think about the possible answer to the third. So that left the second.

She was chewing that over, and not liking it, when Chris said musingly, "You reckon Liddy's done this deliberately. But are you sure? What if it happened by accident? Maybe she doesn't even realize."

Pippa sighed. "Not a chance. I've watched her. She knows what's going on, all right. What I saw out here last night—"

He interrupted, holding up his hands. "OK. I just thought – just hoped. You know."

"Sure," said Pippa sympathetically. "I hoped, too. But it's no use." She shuddered. "And it makes the idea of tackling her about it even scarier."

"We've got to, though, haven't we?"

"Yeah. But how – and when?"

Chris stared around the garden again, frowning. "You said the shadow brought Liddy something. Have you got any idea what it was?"

Pippa shook her head. "I was too far away to see."

"What did she do with it? Put it in her pocket?"

"Probably." Then memory clicked. "No, hang on, she can't have done. She was wearing a sweater and pyjamas, so she wouldn't have *had* any pockets."

"All right. When she came back to the room, was she carrying anything?"

"Only her flute." Pippa suddenly saw where his thoughts were leading, and her eyes lit up. "So whatever it was, she must have hidden it somewhere before she came back."

"Right. And I'd say the most likely place is here, in the garden." Chris paused. "Fancy taking a look around?"

Pippa didn't fancy it, not one bit. But if Chris had the nerve, she wasn't about to admit that she didn't.

She took a deep breath. "Why not?" she said.

They started their search near the statues. Not too near – the stone figure of Lancer made Pippa feel distinctly spooked now, and though he didn't say so, she suspected it was having the same effect on Chris. Besides, all the most likely hiding places were further away, among the overgrown shrubs and bushes.

After ten minutes they'd found only three crisp packets, a drinks can and what looked like a rotting tennis ball. Pippa straightened up, flexing her knees which were getting stiff.

"This is nuts!" she declared. "We don't even know what we're supposed to be looking for.

We might have found it already, and not noticed."

"I don't think so," said Chris.

"Well, if you know something I don't, you'd better tell me. I'm getting fed up."

Chris didn't answer, and she started to feel annoyed. Her head came up. "Chris, I said—"

She stopped. Chris had been pushing his way towards the back of the garden, wading in among the knee-deep undergrowth. Now, he was standing absolutely still, staring down at something.

"What is it?" A nervous edge crept into Pippa's voice.

Chris didn't speak. But he beckoned. On tip-toe (why on *earth* was she doing that? As if something might hear her . . .) Pippa went to join him.

He pointed. "Look."

She did. And her mouth went dry.

The long grass grew very thickly, but a patch of it had been disturbed. In the middle of the patch, as if in a nest, was a collection of bones. The bones formed a pattern. It wasn't complete, but they both recognized it. A skeleton. About the length and shape of a medium-sized dog.

Pippa sucked in a breath, but it seemed to

stick in her throat. "*What* . . ." She couldn't get any further.

"I think," said Chris, "we've found Liddy's secret hoard."

Pippa remembered what she'd seen last night: the spectral dog, bringing something in its mouth. Something for Liddy. A small, pale-coloured object.

Like a bone . . .?

Was Lancer's ghost bringing his own bones back from the grave, and giving them to his new friend?

"It can't be . . ." she mumbled indistinctly. "Oh God, Chris, it *can't!*" She remembered the bone under Jayne's bed – it had been meant for Liddy, it hadn't been put there to scare Jayne at all – and the one in the corridor near their room. She thought she was going to be sick. Swallowing the feeling back, she added, "There's got to be another explanation! A *sane* one!"

Chris nodded. "Yeah . . . yeah, there has. But there's only one person who can tell us what it is." He started to reach towards the bones, then changed his mind. "There's a lot of it missing," he added.

"I know."

"The skull, for a start. Bits of the legs. The ribcage isn't—"

"I *know*! Don't tell me!" Pippa squirmed. "The thing is, *why's* he doing this?"

Before Chris could come up with any sort of answer, a noise of chattering voices interrupted, and a group of their schoolmates appeared at the top of the steps.

"Quick!" Chris hissed. "Cover it up – they mustn't see!"

Hastily they pushed and folded the long grass blades back over the grisly sight, then, trying to look casual, strolled to meet the newcomers.

"You two're around early," someone said. "What's up, concert nerves?"

"Oh, no!" Pippa whispered. She'd completely forgotten that the first concert was tonight. "We'll be rehearsing all day – there won't be *time* to talk to Liddy!"

"Then it'll have to wait!" Chris hissed back. "Shh, or the others'll hear!" Raising his voice he said cheerfully, "Yeah, concert nerves. Same as you lot by the look of it, or you wouldn't be out of bed either! Hey, you know that bit in 'The Four Seasons', where it gets really tricky. . ."

Pippa watched as, skilfully, he started to steer everyone back the way they'd come. She glanced over her shoulder, but the skeleton was well hidden. Pippa shivered. Then, suddenly realizing that she didn't want to be left alone in the garden, she ran to catch up with Chris.

12

Jayne didn't come down to breakfast. According to Mr Elwood – who was on a very short fuse this morning – she was having melo-dramatic fits all over the place, and refusing to play in the concert. Ms Lane was trying to "talk some sense into her", but so far she hadn't had much success.

"You're her friend, Pippa," said Mr Elwood tetchily. "Maybe you'd better have a go."

Pippa protested that she certainly *wasn't* any friend of Jayne's but Mr Elwood wouldn't listen. And he wouldn't take no for an answer.

"All right, Mr Elwood, I'll try," Pippa said at last, reluctantly. "But I don't suppose it'll work."

"Something's got to!" Mr Elwood said through clenched teeth. "I've had just about enough of these stupid tantrums. Ghosts and ghouls in her bedroom, indeed! She's been reading too many horror stories, and it's nothing but her own ridiculous imagination."

Pippa glanced down the table to where Liddy was picking at her breakfast. She didn't seem to be listening, but you could never tell. What was *she* going to do today? Would she go back to the sunken garden? Did she have any more bones to add to her collection . . .?

"Right!" Mr Elwood stood up. "Jayne or no Jayne, we've got a concert to play in tonight. Rehearsal in the small hall at eleven, another quick run-through at three o'clock, then early tea before the coach comes at six to take you all to the church."

"Church?" Pippa said, and he gave her a withering look.

"Yes, Pippa, church. Tonight's concert's in the church at Low Aspen. Don't you *ever* listen to what I say?"

Pippa gulped. She'd known, of course, but it had gone completely out of her mind. The church. Where Lancer's grave was. *Uh-oh* . . .

People were finishing their food and clearing plates away. Liddy got up – in a hurry, it seemed – and left the hall, and Pippa wanted to go after her and find out what she was up to. But as she got hastily to her feet, Mr Elwood stopped her.

"Pippa, you'd better go and talk to Jayne now, and see what you can do. She's in Ms Lane's room." Pippa dithered, and he added impatiently, "Well, go on, get on with it. We haven't got all day!"

She couldn't argue. She tried to signal with her eyebrows to Chris, hoping that he'd follow Liddy, but she didn't know if he understood. With a sigh, she went out of the hall and headed for the stairs.

Ms Lane was only too glad to leave Pippa alone with Jayne. Jayne looked terrible – white as a sheet, and puffy-eyed as if she'd been crying for hours.

"I'm *not* going to play tonight!" she declared. "How *can* I, after what I've been through? You don't *understand*!"

"No, I don't," said Pippa. "Because you haven't told me properly what happened."

Jayne shuddered theatrically. "I can't tell you! I can't even bear to *think* about it!"

"Well, I'm not going to understand anything unless you do, am I? Come on, Jayne. Try."

"You won't believe me!"

There was a pause. Then Pippa said, "Oh, but I might. I just might."

She hadn't really meant to say it, and she knew it might be a big mistake. But the words were out now. And Jayne was staring at her with sudden intense curiosity.

"What do you mean?" she said.

Pippa didn't have much choice. She'd started this now, so she had to see it through.

"OK," she said, very quietly. "You woke up and heard something moving around by your bed, right?"

A nod. Jayne's face was frozen.

"Was it . . ." Pippa swallowed. "Was it the same thing that's been following you since two days after we got here?"

This time the silence seemed to last for ever. Then, in a tiny whisper, Jayne said, "*How do you know?*"

"Because I've seen it, too."

Jayne continued to stare at her for a few moments. Then, suddenly and violently, she burst into tears.

"Oh, Pippa!" she sobbed. "Then it isn't just me! Oh, Pippa . . . oh, please, please, you've got to help me. Oh, you will, won't you? Oh, *Pippa* . . ."

All Pippa's dislike of Jayne was swept away

by a wave of pity. Jayne wasn't arrogant, conceited or catty any more. She was just an ordinary person, who was scared half out of her mind.

"Come on," she said kindly, putting an arm round Jayne's shoulders. "Of course I'll help you. Have a good cry, then when you feel better, we'll talk. All right?"

Jayne nodded, snivelling. "Yes . . . oh, yes." Then, weakly, she added two words that she'd probably hardly ever said before in her life.

"Thank you!"

"Well?" demanded Mr Elwood when Pippa walked into the rehearsal room at eleven o'clock. "Have you managed it?"

Pippa nodded. "She'll play, Mr Elwood."

"That's a relief!" He looked around. "Where is she, then?"

Pippa sighed. "I couldn't get her to come to rehearsal. She's really tired, so I said she'd better sleep for a bit."

"Hmpf." Mr Elwood grunted. "I suppose that'll have to be good enough." Then he relented. "All right, Pippa. Well done. Now go to your place and let's get started."

Pippa sat down. She could have slept for about twelve hours herself; her eyelids felt as if they were made of lead, and if she yawned she was sure half her head would fall off. But she'd achieved what she set out to do. And she'd learned quite a lot.

When she finally stopped crying, Jayne had blurted out everything. She'd first seen the shadowy dog on the day Pippa and the others had gone to Low Aspen, and since then it had seemed to latch on to her, following her wherever she went. She glimpsed it on the stairs, in passages, outside in the gardens – even, briefly, in the disco, among all the flashing lights and dancing people. It haunted her in the nightmares she had, and no matter how hard she tried, she couldn't shake it off. That, she admitted, was why she'd freaked when she found the bone under her bed. Dogs – bones. The connection seemed obvious.

And it had all started when she'd had that row with Liddy in the garden, and shoved Liddy's flute into the stone statue's mouth.

Jayne believed that she'd somehow disturbed Lancer's ghost, and now it was angry with her. Pippa knew there was a lot more to it than that, but she hadn't said so. This situation needed *very* careful handling. So she certainly hadn't mentioned the half-complete skeleton in the garden, or the ruined tights and music sheet that Chris had found. And she hadn't brought Liddy into it. All she'd said was that she, too, believed in the ghost, and that she'd do whatever she could to help Jayne shake it off.

The next thing, now, was to confront Liddy. The only likely chance today would be after lunch, so if she could nab Chris –

"Hello?" said Mr Elwood's sarcastic voice. "Is there anybody in there, Pippa?"

Pippa blinked and shook her head. "Uh?"

Mr Elwood sighed. "Wake up! And *if* you don't mind, maybe we can get some work done!"

"Sorry," Pippa mumbled, wishing the whole world would just go away. She picked up her violin. "I'm ready now."

The rehearsal seemed to go on for ever, but finally Mr Elwood was satisfied, and called a halt. As they were all packing up their instruments, Chris edged his way over to Pippa. Checking that Liddy wasn't in earshot, he said, "I've got something to tell you."

Pippa opened her mouth to ask what it was, and was hit by an enormous yawn.

"You look wiped out," said Chris.

"So would you be if you hadn't had any

sleep at all last night." She rubbed her eyes, which were trying to close by themselves. "What's happened?"

"Well, I saw what you were trying to tell me at breakfast, when old misery-guts sent you to talk to Jayne. So I followed Liddy."

Pippa livened up a bit. "Yeah?"

"She went to the sunken garden. I hid behind one of those pillars and watched her. She went to where the bones are, and she put something else there. I think Lancer's brought her another one."

"Did you get a closer look?"

"No." He shook his head. "Someone else came out, and I didn't want to be seen hanging around, so I went. Haven't had a chance to go back yet."

She chewed her lip. "Do you think Liddy suspected anything? That the grass had been disturbed?"

"Don't think so. She didn't act like it, anyway; so I reckon – hey, watch out, she's heading this way!"

Liddy was moving towards them. She didn't look interested in their talk, but neither of them was about to take any chances.

". . . See you at lunch?" Chris said more loudly.

"Er – yeah, right," Pippa replied. "I'll probably grab a sarnie and take it out to the garden."

"Oh, right. I might do the same, then. Get a bit of fresh air." It was a coded way of arranging to meet up again, and with a casual wave Pippa left the rehearsal room. She'd go upstairs and put her violin away, then with any luck she and Chris could talk properly.

But Pippa had reckoned without her own weariness. She only meant to sit down on the bed for long enough to change her hot trainers for sandals. But the bed was comfortable, and the room was drowsily warm . . . *Just a couple of minutes,* she told herself, lying back. Her eyelids drooped. Her body relaxed. She fell soundly asleep.

And came out of a dream to find Liddy shaking her shoulder.

"Pippa! Pippa, wake up!" Liddy's face swam into view as Pippa opened bleary eyes. "It's gone three. Mr Elwood's doing his crust, and he sent me to look for you."

Gone three – *oh hell* Pippa thought. *The afternoon rehearsal!* She was furious with herself – she'd completely blown the chance to talk to Chris, and now there'd be no time before the concert.

"Come on," Liddy urged, "or I'll be in trouble, too."

"All right, I'm coming." Pippa heaved herself off the bed, grabbed her violin case, and followed Liddy out of the door.

She got another chewing out from Mr Elwood, and accusing looks from Chris that clearly said, "Where *were* you?" But at least she felt less tired. If she was going to think straight for the rest of the day, that was some consolation.

She tried to get Chris on his own after the run-through, but it proved impossible, largely thanks to Jayne. Jayne came downstairs for the hasty meal before the coach arrived to pick them up. She was still very quiet and subdued, and didn't revel in the fact that everyone was being nice to her. Instead, she latched on to Pippa like a twin. Pippa knew why she was doing it, and sympathized. But it didn't help the situation at all.

At six o'clock, three coaches, two carrying orchestras and one a school choir, set off in convoy for Low Aspen. Chris was in the seat in front of Pippa, but as Jayne was squashed in next to her, it was still impossible to say anything in private. In the town, bunting had been put up for the festival, and a banner was draped along the churchyard wall announcing tonight's concert. The convoy stopped, and as they all climbed out, Pippa peered uneasily towards the graves of Nathaniel Thornbury and Lancer. She could only see the tops of the stones from here. They didn't *look* any different.

Then, near the graves, something moved.

Pippa stopped dead, staring. She tried to tell herself it was just a cloud-shadow, but cloud shadows weren't that small. And they didn't slink furtively over the ground, like an animal that didn't want to be seen.

Besides, that shadow had been just a little bit too *solid*.

"What's the matter?" Jayne, at Pippa's shoulder, hissed anxiously. "What are you looking at?"

"What? Oh – er – nothing." Pippa turned a bright, false smile on her . . . then saw Chris standing a few paces away. Saw his expression. He, too, had noticed the shadow by the graves. And he was thinking exactly the same thing as she was.

"Come on, Pippa, move!" Mr Elwood's impatient voice broke the spell suddenly. "You're holding everyone up!"

Pippa started towards the church. But as she

walked up the path, with her schoolmates chattering around her, she couldn't shake off the feeling that something dark and unpleasant and hostile was watching her go.

13

All through the first part of the concert, Pippa was like a cat on hot bricks. She couldn't concentrate on the music. All she could think about was Lancer. She kept believing she saw the shadow-dog again, gliding by the wall, lurking behind the end of a pew, creeping slowly and stealthily among the orchestra. It was only her imagination, overworking in the low light of the church. But it rattled her badly.

Then there was Liddy. Even from a distance Pippa could tell that Liddy was keyed-up and excited. Her playing was intense, all her movements quick and jerky, and there was a peculiar, bright glint in her eyes. She, too, kept

119

sneaking glances around, as if she was waiting for something that she was sure would arrive before too long.

The concert was in two parts, and in the last piece before the interval Liddy had a short solo. The moment came: she drew breath, started to play – and Pippa felt a clutching sensation in her stomach. Because Liddy had added something new to the solo. A little trill, coldly and eerily haunting, shivering down the scale before she launched into the proper melody.

Pippa had heard those notes before. In the garden. The trill was Liddy's call to Lancer.

The piece ended, there was applause and they stood up and bowed. Pippa all but ran from the platform, giving Jayne the slip and rushing to find Chris.

"Did you hear?" she hissed, grabbing his arm. "Those extra notes – do you know what they were?"

"Yeah." Chris's face was grim. "And I think we should – uh-oh. Here comes Jayne. Quick, before she sees us!"

They dodged behind the screen that had been put up to separate the audience from the performers, and slipped out of the church by a side door. In the churchyard, Chris said, "I think we ought to take another look at Lancer's grave."

After what she'd seen earlier, Pippa didn't like the idea. But Chris was already striding off, so she told herself not to be chicken and followed him across the grass. The sun was setting, and in the gathering gloom the tombstones of Nathaniel and his dog looked pale and spectral. Then, as they approached the graves, Chris stopped and sniffed.

"Can you smell anything?"

Pippa sniffed, too. "Ugh! Like something gone mouldy."

"Right. Now ask yourself where you've smelled it before."

She frowned – then memory clicked. "When Jayne freaked out last night! It's exactly the same smell that was in our room!"

"Bullseye," said Chris. "Come on. Let's see what's been going on."

He set off again, but Pippa had a sudden bout of nerves. She hung back, peering around uneasily as Chris went towards the stones. He reached them. Stopped. Stared down. Then he turned and beckoned urgently.

"Pippa! You'd better come and look at this!"

Pippa's heart thumped, hard and painfully. She ran to join him, and he pointed.

The earth at the foot of Lancer's gravestone had been disturbed. It looked freshly turned, as if something had been digging there.

And lying on the soft brown heap of soil were five more bones.

"Oh, my God," Pippa whispered. "More of the skeleton . . . It *is* Lancer. It's *got* to be!"

"Looks like it," Chris said softly. "And see those marks in the earth?"

"Claws!" So the crazy, horrible theory was right. Piece by piece, bone by bone, the shadow-dog was digging up his own mortal remains.

And then the worst thought of all came to Pippa. It looked as if the bones would go on appearing until the skeleton was complete. So what would happen then . . .?

She opened her mouth to voice the question to Chris – and stopped as she heard a sound in the distance behind them. *Footsteps*, her mind warned.

"Chris, someone's coming!"

"Quick!" He grabbed her arm. "Over there, by the yew hedge – get out of sight." He gave her a shove to start her on her way. Then, to her horror, he bent and snatched up one of the bones from the pile.

"*No!*" Pippa hissed. "*Don't touch them!*"

122

Chris ignored her protest and ran for the hedge, towing her with him. They ducked into the enclosing darkness, and as they dropped to a crouch Pippa said frantically, "For God's sake, put it back!"

"Shh! Keep your voice down!" He peered back towards the graves. "Anyway, it's too late. Look."

A figure was approaching through the dusk. It was Liddy, as they'd both known it would be. Hurrying. Furtive. She reached the graves, and they heard her gasp of excitement.

"Yes!" She reached out eagerly towards the little heap of bones. "I knew you'd do it, Lancer, I knew you would!" The bones made repulsive clicking noises as she scooped them up and put them into her music case. "Four more," she breathed. "It's nearly complete, Lancer! Oh, you wonderful dog!"

In the dark of the yew hedge Pippa and Chris looked at each other and squirmed inwardly. Pippa wanted to jump to her feet, shout and yell at Liddy, shake some sanity into her. She started to get up, but Chris pulled her back.

"Leave it!" he whispered. "This isn't the right place – too many other people around!"

She saw the sense of that and subsided.

Liddy was touching Lancer's tombstone now, stroking it, murmuring something that they couldn't catch. Then, with a final pat, she scrambled to her feet again, turned, and flitted away back to the church.

Very slowly, Pippa and Chris emerged. Pippa felt sick and Chris didn't look much better.

"We'll have to get back, too." The voice that came out of Pippa's mouth didn't sound like her own. "The concert'll be starting again . . ."

Chris swallowed. "Tonight," he said. "Back at the Manor. We'll confront her then. We've *got* to."

She nodded. "Before that skeleton . . ." She stopped.

"I know. Before it gets completed."

They headed back to the church, trying not to let the urge to run get the better of them. But as they went, Pippa thought she heard something else. She told herself she was imagining things again, and she just about managed to believe it.

But if she *hadn't* believed, she'd have said that the noise was coming from the direction of the grave.

And it sounded like a soft, threatening growl.

Coffee and snacks were ready back at the Manor, and everyone sat around chatting about the concert and generally unwinding. Jayne was sticking close to Pippa again, making it impossible for her to talk properly to Chris. But they both kept a sharp eye on Liddy. And when, after about twenty minutes, she slipped out of the refectory, it didn't take Einstein to work out where she was going. Especially as she was still carrying her music case.

Chris left the room a few seconds later, and Pippa turned to Jayne.

"Won't be a minute," she said, and jerked a thumb at the door. "Got to go to the loo."

Luckily, Jayne was telling someone about the wrong notes one of the cellists had played, and she hardly noticed when Pippa left her to it. From the front door Pippa ran round to the side of the house. There was no sign of Liddy, but Chris was there, heading cautiously for the sunken garden. Pippa followed, trying not to make any sound, and caught him up near the top of the steps.

"Great – you got rid of Jayne!" They crouched down behind the pillar, as Pippa had done before. "Liddy's by the statues. She's going to put those new bones with the others. So I think it's time we confronted her."

"She'll run when she sees us," Pippa pointed out.

"We'll come at her from opposite sides." Chris nodded towards the bushes where Pippa had hidden last night. "I'll go round, and use the bushes as cover. When I'm in position, I'll whistle; then you go down the steps, and we'll block her between us." He patted his pocket, checking that the bone he'd taken was still there. "We've got evidence now. We'll get the truth out of her."

He hurried away and melted into the darkness. Pippa waited, tense and nervous. The statues were pale blobs down in the sunken garden, and she thought she could see Liddy's vague shape moving nearby. *Come on, Chris! Or she'll finish what she's doing and go before we can catch her!*

As she thought that, a low, clear whistle rang out. Though she'd been expecting it, it made Pippa jump. Liddy was startled, too. Her head came up sharply; she looked this way and that – then abruptly she began to scramble back through the undergrowth, away from the statues.

Pippa jumped to her feet and ran down the steps. She'd just reached the bottom when Liddy saw her and stopped dead.

"*Ahh!*" She put a hand to her mouth in shock – then recognition dawned. "Pippa! Wh-what are *you* doing here?"

"Coincidence, huh?" said Pippa. "Having fun, are you?"

"I was just – that is, I—"

"Forget it, Liddy," Chris's voice interrupted from behind. "We know what's going on."

Liddy whirled. Chris had come down the slope at the garden's far end, and was walking towards them. He had a torch, and he shone it on Liddy's face. Her cheeks were flaming and she looked alarmed – and guilty.

But she'd also had a few seconds to scramble her wits back together. "Going on?" she echoed. "What do you mean? What are you talking about?"

"We're talking about Lancer," said Pippa. "And some bones." She pointed at the music case in Liddy's hand. "Like the ones you've got in there."

"*What?* That's crazy – there aren't any bones in there!"

"No, there aren't," said Chris. "Because she's already put them with the others."

"Others . . .?" Liddy's horrified expression gave her away, and Chris smiled grimly.

"Let's have a look, shall we, Pippa? See how it's coming along."

He started to walk back to where the skeleton was hidden. For a few moments Liddy stood frozen – then suddenly she darted after him.

"No!" she cried. "Leave it alone! You mustn't, it's mine, it's—"

She stopped. Chris was shining the torch down into the long grass. There lay the skeleton, with the new bones that she'd added tonight. It was almost complete now. Only the skull and one leg bone were missing.

"It's Lancer, isn't it?" said Chris. Liddy didn't speak, and Pippa chimed in, "We know you've called him up. He's out to get Jayne, isn't he? And *you're* making him do it!"

"No . . ." Liddy shook her head violently. "No, it isn't – I didn't – look, I've never seen that before, I don't know where it came from—"

Chris sighed. "It's no good, Liddy. We saw those bones tonight, in the churchyard. We saw you take them, and we heard what you said. Oh, yeah; and you missed one. Cos we got there first."

Fishing in his pocket, he pulled out the bone he'd taken. Liddy stared at it, her eyes widening.

"Give it to me!" Her voice rose to a high, nervous note, and one hand shot out. "*Give* it to me, Chris. *Please*! You mustn't keep it, you can't! Or . . ." The sentence fizzled out and Pippa prompted, "Or what? What'll happen?"

Liddy looked desperately from one to the other of them. Then her face seemed to crumple, and tears welled in her eyes.

"What's the use?" she said, her voice a mixture of anger and misery. "You don't understand – you never would! *No one* understands!"

She spun round, as if she was going to push past them and run back to the Manor. Chris made a grab for her, snatching at her arm –

And jumped back with a yelp as an ugly, threatening snarl sounded from somewhere near their feet.

A black silhouette stood on the path that ran alongside the ornamental pond. It was barring their way, and it held something in its mouth. Something large, pale, and toothily gaping.

Lancer had returned. And he had brought the final part of the skeleton.

His own skull.

"Chris . . ." Pippa's voice shook with fear. "Chris, back off . . . get away from it . . ."

The shadow-dog growled deep in its ghostly

throat. It raised its head – and now it had eyes: hideous red pinpoints that focused malevolently on Chris's face. Then, slowly, it took a step towards him.

"He wants the bone, Chris," said Liddy, sounding strange and not at all like her real self. She looked at the spectre. "Go on, Lancer. Make him give it to you."

The red eyes, like small, hellish fires, returned her gaze. Lancer dropped the skull. It rolled to Liddy's feet, and several teeth fell out with an awful rattle. Liddy smiled, bent down and picked up the skull.

"*Good* boy, Lancer," she said.

The shadow-dog stared at Chris again. Growled again. "Chris, don't be an idiot!" Pippa pleaded. "Give it what it wants!"

"No!" Chris sounded – and looked – scared, but his fist closed tightly round the bone. "It mustn't be completed!"

Desperate, Pippa turned on Liddy. "Call him off!" she shouted. "You started this – make it stop, *now*!"

"He wants his bone," Liddy repeated stubbornly, almost as if she was in a trance. "He's got to have it. I *want* him to have it." Suddenly, violently, she shook off Pippa's clutching hands, and her voice rose to a shout.

"Go on, Lancer, go on! *Get it back!*"

To Pippa's rioting imagination it seemed that time screeched to a halt. There was Liddy, eager and wild-eyed. There was Chris, flinching but still trying to stand his ground. Even Lancer was frozen motionless in his threatening crouch.

But only for an instant before the stillness exploded. Then came a savage snarl, a scream –

And in a blur of deadly ferocity, the ghost-dog launched himself in a flying leap at Chris's throat.

14

"*Chris!*" Pippa didn't even think; she flung herself forward, yelling Chris's name and lashing out wildly at the horror that was attacking him. For three seconds there was mayhem – Lancer snarling and snapping, Chris and Pippa shouting and flailing as they strove to beat him off. Pippa's windmilling arms hit the shadowdog, hit him again – *there was nothing there, but she could FEEL it, hair and skin and muscle*— In the chaos she glimpsed Liddy fleeing, running; then Lancer launched himself at the bone in Chris's hand.

"*Aaah!*" With a bellow of shock and pain Chris lost his balance, cannoned into Pippa, and they both crashed to the ground. Pippa's face went smack into a tussock of grass—

And suddenly there was total, eerie silence.

She raised her head. Liddy was gone. Lancer was gone. She and Chris were alone in the garden.

"Chris!" On hands and knees she crawled over to him. "Are you hurt?"

Chris struggled to a sitting position. "Nnnh . . . No. Don't think so – *oww*!" He gripped one wrist with the other hand, trying to flex the fingers. "Feels like it's twisted. . ."

It was the hand that had held the bone. The hand Lancer had lunged at. "Let me look," said Pippa anxiously. She expected to see blood, torn flesh. There was nothing. No mark at all.

But the bone wasn't there. Lancer had got what he wanted.

"Come on." Pippa climbed unsteadily to her feet, then reached to haul him up, too. "Let's get the hell out of this place!"

"No, hang on." Chris looked around. "Where's my torch?"

"I don't know and I don't care!" They'd probably trampled it to bits in the scrimmage, Pippa thought. "Leave it!"

But Chris wouldn't. "I've got to find that bone!" he said. "Don't you see? That and the skull – they're probably the last ones Liddy needed to make the skeleton complete!"

"So *what?*"

"So what happens when it *is* complete?"

Pippa's eyes widened. In the churchyard earlier she'd asked herself the same question, but had forgotten all about it. Now, though . . .

"Lancer's still just a ghost," Chris went on ominously. "That's why he couldn't do any real damage when he attacked me. But when he's got his whole skeleton back . . ."

"That might change." Pippa finished the sentence for him.

"Yeah. He might *really* come alive."

Pippa hugged herself to stop a sudden bout of shivering, and stared around the dark garden. "Surely he can't, can he?" she protested, appalled. "Not properly. I mean . . . he's been dead more than a hundred years! It's unnatural; it's – it's all *wrong!*"

"Liddy doesn't think so," said Chris.

Pippa saw the whole ugly picture. Liddy desperately wanted a dog of her own. She'd rescued a stray, but her parents wouldn't let her keep it. So now she'd found another one. One that nobody could take away from her.

Because nobody would dare try.

Faithful Beyond Death. Oh yes, Lancer

was faithful, all right. If someone upset his new mistress – as Jayne had done – he didn't like it *at all*.

And if he came fully, *physically* back to life, how much more of a threat would he be?

"Liddy can't understand what she's doing," Pippa whispered. "She *can't*!"

"I don't think she does," said Chris soberly. "All she cares about is having Lancer for her friend. She probably doesn't even know that he's out to get Jayne." He laughed ruefully. "And us, too, now."

"We've got to tell her!"

"Sure. But will she listen?"

"She'll have to!" Pippa swallowed. "Cos I've got an awful feeling, Chris. If that skeleton gets completed . . . if it does, then I don't think *any-one*'ll be able to control Lancer. Not even Liddy!"

Chris nodded grim agreement. "At least it isn't complete yet," he said. "Liddy's got the skull. She took it when she ran off. So we've got to find her, and stop her putting it with the other bones." He swung round, frustrated. "We need some light! Look, Pippa, there's sure to be another torch around in the Manor. If you go and get one, I'll stay here in case Liddy comes back."

She was horrified. "I'm not leaving you here on your own! What if Lancer—"

"Lancer can't do anything really dangerous till that skeleton's finished. I'll be OK. Just *go*!"

Pippa wanted to tell him a dozen different reasons why she wasn't going to do any such thing. Instead, she stood silent for a single moment – then turned and pelted away towards the brick steps.

"Lancer? Are you there, Lancer?"

Liddy's cautious whisper mingled with the rustle of leaves in the bushes as the breeze stirred them. There was no answer. She hadn't expected one, not yet. But she knew that Lancer had sensed her. He would come back. Soon.

On hands and knees she moved to the edge of the shrubbery and peered round it to the sunken garden. She could see Chris's silhouette in the gloom; he was standing by the statues, and he looked restless. *Go away*, Liddy thought furiously. *Go away, and leave us alone*! She'd seen Pippa running towards the Manor, but didn't know whether she'd return. Not that it mattered. Lancer could frighten them away. And when they'd gone, all she had to do was go back to the garden and finish what she'd begun.

Behind her, a small patch of darkness moved. Liddy didn't see it. But she heard the low, throaty *huff*, and quickly she looked over her shoulder.

"Lancer." Her face broke into a strange, slow smile. The shadow-dog *huff*ed again. He came closer, and she saw that he had something in his mouth. Very carefully, he laid it at her feet.

It was the bone he'd snatched from Chris. The last bone of all.

"Good boy," said Liddy fondly. "*Good* boy!"

Pippa eased through the front door and looked around the entrance hall. She could hear the sound of chatter from the refectory, but there was no one in sight. Good. Now, one likely place to find a torch would be behind the reception desk . . .

To her huge relief, there *was* a torch, and a powerful one, too. Grabbing it, she straightened up.

And came face to face with Jayne.

"Pippa!" Jayne looked distinctly antsy. "Where have you *been*?" Then she saw the torch. "What's that for?"

"I – er – something I've got to do," Pippa said hastily. "Won't take long."

Jayne's face fell. "But I want to go upstairs, and I'm scared to go on my own! You've got to come with me, Pippa!"

"Not now!" Pippa told her. "Find someone else."

Maybe her face gave her away, or the tone of her voice. Whichever it was, Jayne realized that something was very wrong.

"What's going on?" she said, her voice suddenly dangerously high-pitched. "What's happened? Something has, I know, I can see! It's the ghost, isn't it? Tell me, Pippa! *Tell me!*"

"Jayne," Pippa said through clenched teeth, "you do *not* want to know, believe me! Stay here; don't do anything. I'll explain when I get back."

"No!" cried Jayne. "You've got to tell me now, or I'll start imagining the worst things in the world!"

"I *can't!*" Pippa insisted. "Chris is waiting, and if I don't—"

"*Chris?* What's he got to do with it?"

Pippa hadn't meant to let that particular cat out of the bag but any more arguing would waste precious time.

"Look," she said, "I'm going, *now.*"

She tried to barge past, but Jayne blocked

the way and grabbed hold of both her arms.

"You're not going anywhere until you've told me!" said Jayne ferociously. "And if you don't – if you don't, I'm going to start screaming. *Very* loudly!"

"Come on, Pippa, come on!" Chris hissed the words under his breath, hopping from one foot to the other. Where was she? She shouldn't be taking this long. Though nothing had happened, he was getting nervous. Liddy was around somewhere, he felt sure of it. And wherever Liddy was, you could bet Lancer wouldn't be far away.

"Come *on*, Pippa!" And he thought: maybe she'd run into someone. Maybe Mr Elwood had seen her, and she couldn't get away . . .

He could go back to the Manor and look for her. But if he did, there'd be no one to watch the garden. Chris dithered. Maybe if he went to the top of the steps, he could at least see whether she was coming.

He set off, hurrying, along the path, and ran up the steps. No sign of anyone. No, hang on, what was that? Someone coming round the side of the house.

Two people.

"Oh, no!" The Manor's outside security light

was on, and Chris could see Pippa clearly now, with Jayne right behind her.

With a sinking feeling, he started to run to meet them.

Pippa saw Chris coming and put on a spurt. She heard Jayne wail, "Wait for *meee!*" but ignored her, and slid to a panting halt as Chris came up.

"What the heck's *she* doing here?" Chris demanded.

"I couldn't stop her!" Pippa gasped. "She saw me, and she started asking questions, and when I tried to get away she—"

"Chris!" Jayne had caught them up. "Oh, Chris, what's *happening*? Pippa won't tell me!"

"Just *leave* it, will you?" Pippa snarled.

Jayne began arguing, and more seconds were wasted before Chris cut in. "There isn't time for all this! Liddy's probably in the garden now—"

"Liddy?" Jayne's voice nearly shot off the scale, and Pippa turned on her.

"Yes, Liddy!" She whirled again. "Come on, Chris, let's go. If Jayne wants to follow us, that's her funeral!"

She took off again, racing for the sunken garden with Chris at her heels. Jayne shouted,

"Come back!" Then, realizing that they weren't going to, she pounded after them.

But Liddy had got there first.

As soon as she reached the top of the steps, Pippa saw the dark figure crouching in the undergrowth near the statues. She punched the torch on and the beam stabbed into the night, lighting Liddy's face as she looked up.

"She's got the skull!" Chris said.

"Liddy, don't!" Pippa cried. "Put it down!"

"Go away!" Liddy shouted back. "It's nothing to do with you!" She scrambled deeper into the undergrowth, parting the grass with quick, frantic hands. White bone glimmered in the torch beam, then she pushed the skull in among the rest of the skeleton.

"There!" she exulted. "It's all here!" She jumped to her feet. "Lancer! Come on, boy, come on! It's finished, and we're ready!" And, putting her fingers in her mouth, she let out a piercing whistle.

"No!" Pippa's yell of protest cut through the whistle as she rushed down the steps and ran at Liddy. Liddy came to meet her, barring her way to the bones, and they slid to a halt face to face.

"Liddy," said Pippa, "you've got to stop this! You mustn't bring Lancer back to life. It's wrong. It's *dangerous*!"

141

Liddy looked away. "He's my friend!" she said defiantly. "And he's a *real* friend, not like any of you! Go away, Pippa. Just go away, and leave us alone!"

"You . . ." The new voice made them both turn quickly. It was Jayne. She'd followed Pippa, and now she stood a few paces away on the path. Her face was ashen and Pippa realized that she'd heard everything – and put two and two together.

"*You* set it on me, didn't you?" One shaky hand came up and pointed accusingly at Liddy. "That ghost, that – that *thing*. *You* called it up, to get back at me!"

"Jayne—" Pippa began.

"Shut up. This is between me and her." Jayne's fear had disappeared under an avalanche of anger, and she took another step towards Liddy. "Answer me, Liddy Kovak! Tell the truth!"

Liddy shrugged, but she wouldn't meet Jayne's eyes. "He's my friend," she said again, sulkily. "If someone's horrible to me and he doesn't like it, that's not my fault." Now she did look at Jayne, and her expression was sly. "He wants to do things for me, that's all. In fact he'll do anything I tell him to."

Chris said suddenly and warningly, "Pippa. . ."

She saw the movement at the same instant. And she heard the small, furtive noise. A *click-click-click*. As if a lot of small, hard objects were rattling and connecting together . . .

Then, from the long grass behind Liddy, came a low, deep-throat and ominous growl.

Pippa swung the torch – and the beam lit him up like a spotlight. Lancer. But he was no longer just a silhouette. Because, through the blackness of his shadow, she could see the outlines of bones. A stench hit her: the smell of something mouldering, that should have stayed buried deep underground. And the ghost-dog, that was no longer just a ghost, opened his jaws to reveal a mouthful of sharp – and very real – teeth.

Lancer's head turned as he looked at them one by one, and again Pippa heard the horrible clicking as bones ground together. Then the monstrous red eyes fixed on just one person. Lancer growled a second time.

And slowly, awkwardly, as if he hadn't *quite* got used to his new, solid reality, he lumbered menacingly forward.

Straight towards Jayne.

15

"No . . ." Jayne stumbled backwards, almost tripping over. "No, don't – Liddy, stop it! *Call it off!*"

Liddy only smiled. "He won't hurt you," she said, in the strange, sing-song tone Pippa had heard her use before. "Not unless I tell him to."

"You're crazy!" All Jayne's self-righteous fury had vanished, and her eyes bulged with fright. "*Stop* it, will you? Make it get away from me!"

But Pippa saw that Liddy wasn't crazy. Her smile, her voice – it was as if she was in a trance. As if something else was controlling her. And Pippa knew what that something was.

"Liddy," she said, very carefully, as if she was talking to a little kid, "Liddy, listen to me. You don't want Lancer to hurt Jayne, do you?"

Liddy frowned uncertainly. "She was horrible to me . . ."

"I know she was. But she's sorry. Aren't you, Jayne?"

"Yes!" Jayne agreed desperately. "I'm sorry, Liddy, I'm sorry, I'm *really* sorry!"

"So tell Lancer, Liddy," Pippa said soothingly. Chris was watching, holding his breath, and she threw him a frantic, meaningful look. She hoped and prayed he'd get the message. "Tell him to leave Jayne alone," she went on. "He's a good dog, isn't he? He's faithful to you. He'll do whatever you say."

"Yes . . ." said Liddy dazedly.

"Well, then. Go on, Liddy. Tell him."

Liddy swallowed. Lancer shuffled another pace towards Jayne. And Chris, unseen by anyone but Pippa, bent down and picked up a broken branch that was lying in the grass . . .

Lancer took another step. Liddy said, "I don't . . ." and frowned again.

"Please, Liddy," Pippa entreated. "*I* haven't been horrible to you, have I?"

"No-o . . ."

"Then do it for me. *Please*?"

Lancer snarled, showing his teeth again. He was closing in on Jayne, who was far too terrified to move a muscle. Still frowning, Liddy looked down at him. She seemed to be mentally struggling with herself. From the corner of her eye Pippa saw Chris take a firmer grip on the branch.

Then Liddy said, in a very small voice, "Lancer. Leave her alone."

She expected Lancer to obey. But he didn't. He kept advancing on Jayne, slowly still, but with deadly intensity. He was slavering now, and a rope of saliva hung down from his jaws.

"Lancer?" Liddy looked confused. "Leave her, Lancer! *Good* boy."

Lancer wasn't interested. He started to growl, then lowered his head menacingly. His body dropped into a crouch – he was preparing to spring –

"*Pippa-a-a* . . ." Jayne whimpered.

Lancer lunged.

He hit Jayne full on in a clumsy, lurching rush. The impact knocked her backwards, and her shriek rang through the garden as she crashed to the ground. Pippa heard Lancer's teeth clashing, saw Jayne's arms and legs flailing; then suddenly Liddy was rushing into the mêlée.

146

"Lancer!" she cried. "Lancer, stop it! No, Lancer, NO!" She made a wild grab for the dog – and with a snarl Lancer twisted around. His jaws parted, he lunged again – and his teeth slashed at Liddy's arm.

"*Ahh!*" Liddy recoiled with a yell of shock and pain, and Pippa saw to her horror that blood was streaming down her wrist. *That bite had been real!*

"*Bad dog!*" Liddy was sobbing and shouting at the same time, doubled over and clutching at her arm. "*Bad, BAD dog!*"

She lurched towards him, as if she was going to hit him. Lancer snarled again, challengingly. Then he whirled, and launched a renewed attack on the screaming Jayne, snapping for her legs.

"*Lancer!*" Liddy cried desperately. Pippa was shouting too; she ran forward, wanting to help, to stop this, to *do* something –

"Get back!" It was Chris's voice, and as Pippa swerved he ran at Lancer, swinging the branch like a baseball bat. The dog saw what was going to happen. With a third snarl, harsh and savage, he tried to turn on Chris. But he wasn't fast enough. The heavy branch sliced through the air and came thwacking down on his shoulders with all the force Chris could give it.

A hideous, unearthly howl rang out, and as the noise whirled past her Pippa heard another and even uglier sound – a splintering, snapping *crack*. The head and body of Lancer's skeleton parted as the branch smashed right through the ancient bones, and the skull hurtled away. It hit the path, ricocheted, bounced again, teeth rattling like castanets –

And came down, turning over and over, to plummet with a smacking splash into the middle of the ornamental pond.

For an appalling moment the headless skeleton stayed rigid, frozen in its last attacking pose. Then, like a slow motion movie, it started to sag. It lost its shape, caved in on itself . . . and collapsed in a lifeless heap of fragments.

And the black shadow that had been the spirit of Lancer had vanished without trace.

Liddy stood like a shop window dummy, staring down at the piled bones. Her mouth trembled, and her voice came out in a tiny quaver.

"No . . . oh, no . . ." She covered her face with her hands and burst into tears. Jayne was crying, too, much more noisily. Pippa thought she should help her, then saw that Chris was already there. So instead she went slowly, shakily over to Liddy.

"I didn't mean to . . ." Liddy mumbled indistinctly. "I didn't think he'd . . . I thought he was – was *faithful* . . ."

"Oh, he was," said Pippa, breathing deeply. "*Too* faithful."

Liddy's hands slid away and she looked bewildered. "Wh-what do you mean?"

Pippa knew she should have been unforgivingly furious with Liddy. She wasn't, though. She pitied her. "You called him up," she said. "I don't know how; maybe it was your flute, that time at rehearsal, after what Jayne did. But he latched on to you. And if anyone upset you, he was out to get them. Only he took it much too far." She glanced over her shoulder, to where Chris was helping Jayne to her feet. "He got *fixed* on things. First on you, then on getting revenge on Jayne. While he was just a ghost, he couldn't do a lot of damage. But once that skeleton was complete . . ."

Liddy blinked slowly. "He hurt me," she said. "When I tried to stop him."

"Yeah, he did. Cos even though you were supposed to be his friend, you got in the way of what he wanted to do. Like I said, he was fixed." Pippa ran her tongue over very dry lips. "He'd have killed Jayne, if he could. You know that, don't you?"

149

"Yes," Liddy whispered.

Pippa could have added, "And maybe he'd have killed anyone else who got in his way. Even you." But she didn't. Liddy knew the truth without needing to be told. The spell Lancer had cast on her was broken. He was gone. And Pippa was certain that he wouldn't be back.

From the gloom Chris spoke. "I'm taking Jayne back to the house." A pause. "You two going to be all right?"

"Sure," said Pippa, and choked back a hysterical giggle. "What about . . .?" She pointed at the heap of bones.

"We'll bury them here in the garden," said Chris. "Tomorrow."

"Yeah. But the skull . . ."

"Leave it. We'd probably never be able to fish it up again, anyway."

"Right." Let it stay at the bottom of the pond, Pippa thought. It was the safest place.

She watched Chris shepherd Jayne away. When she turned back, Liddy was staring at the statues.

"I really thought he was my friend," she whispered.

Pippa sighed. "I think he wanted to be," she replied. "But . . ." Then the words tailed off as she thought, *Oh, what do I know? Maybe he was. Maybe he was the best friend Liddy ever had.*

Liddy walked slowly to the statues. She stretched out the arm that had been bitten, and laid her hand on the stone dog's head.

"Poor Lancer," she murmured sadly. "He did *try*, didn't he?"

A trickle of blood dripped on to the statue, and Pippa shuddered.

"Come on, Liddy," she said. "Let's get you indoors and clean your arm up."

Liddy looked uneasily at her. "You won't tell them? Mr Elwood and the others – you won't tell them what I did?"

"Course I won't. None of us will." No one would believe them anyway, Pippa thought. But things weren't going to be quite the same from now on. Jayne'd get over it. She was the type. In a few weeks she'd probably convince herself that none of it had ever happened. Liddy, though . . . she was different.

But maybe, Pippa thought, she could help a bit. A dog, two cats and four rabbits added up to a lot of pets for one household. A bit of help looking after them and playing with them might be quite a sensible idea . . .

"Come on," she said again, and put an arm

round Liddy's shoulders. "We've got another concert tomorrow. You're not going to chicken out on us, are you?"

For a moment Liddy stood very still, as if she was going to argue. Then, suddenly, she relaxed.

"No," she said. In the dark, Pippa could still see the glint of tears in her eyes. But then she wiped them away, and almost managed to smile.

"Goodbye, Lancer," she said.

And she let Pippa lead her out of the garden.

Well, it was all over. And not just the music festival, Pippa thought as she peered through the coach window for her very last glimpse of Aspen Manor.

"Sorry to be going?" asked Chris, who was sitting beside her.

"Umm . . . no." Pippa grinned, then sighed. "I could sleep for a week!"

"Tell me about it! Still, it was good, wasn't it?" He struck a Mr Elwood-like pose. "A triumph!"

She grinned. "The music, you mean?"

"What else? Go on then, go to sleep. I'll wake you up when we get home."

Pippa leaned back and shut her eyes. Liddy

was sitting somewhere at the back. She probably wasn't talking to anyone. She was probably going to sleep, too. And Jayne had gone back four days ago, stricken with a sudden "bug". No one had really missed her, and by the time term started again she'd be back to her old bumptious self. She'd never talk to Liddy again, but that wouldn't be much of a loss to either of them. And there wouldn't be any more nasty remarks or dirty tricks. Lancer had achieved that much.

It was really, truly *over*.

The coach swung out of the drive gates and headed for the main road that led to the city. Back at the Manor, in the gravelled courtyard, three more coaches were waiting to carry their passengers away. One group – a school choir – were having a last walk around, enjoying the sunshine while they waited for their driver to finish his lunch. And four of them had wandered down to the sunken garden.

They looked at the pool, watched the dragonflies and water-boatmen for a bit, then went and sat down in the grass, near the statues.

"Pompous type, wasn't he?" someone commented, looking up at the stone image of Nathaniel Thornbury. "Really fancied himself."

"He looks like the Head," said someone else, and they all laughed.

"What about his dog, then?" said a third person. "My aunt and uncle had one of those bull terrier things. It kept chasing the postman, and he wouldn't deliver their letters any more till they got rid of it."

"Brilliant!" said a girl with long, blonde hair. "I'd like a dog like that. Then I could set it on my kid sister – with any luck, it'd eat her!" She turned round and peered at the plinth. "What was he called? Oh, yeah; Lancer. Well, hi, Lancer!" She patted the statue. "Going to come home with me, then, and sort our Kerry out? Good boy, huh?" And she whistled shrilly between her teeth.

"Come on, you lot!" yelled their choir teacher from the top of the steps. "Time to go!"

They went, still chattering, not in any hurry. The coach's engine had started up, thrumming and kicking out exhaust fumes. They piled on board. The blonde girl grabbed a window seat and flopped cheerfully into it. The doors hissed, and started to close.

And no one noticed the small black shadow that darkened the steps. Hovered. As if it was thinking.

Then flowed like water on to the coach, to merge with the more *natural* shadows under the blonde girl's feet.